M

DATE DUE

	JUN 1 0 2008
NOV 1 6 2004	
MAR 1 7 2005	
APR 1 3 2005	
JUN 0 8 2005	
JUN 1 7 2005	
JUN 3 0 2005	
NOV 1 4 2007	

DEMCO, INC. 38-2931

CREATCH BATTLER

Also by Mark Crilley

Akiko on the Planet Smoo

Akiko in the Sprubly Islands

Akiko and the Great Wall of Trudd

Akiko in the Castle of Alia Rellapor

Akiko and the Intergalactic Zoo

Akiko and the Alpha Centauri 5000

Akiko and the Journey to Toog

BILLY CLIKK

CREATCH BATTLER

Mark Crilley

Delacorte Press

Published by
Delacorte Press
an imprint of
Random House Children's Books
a division of Random House, Inc.
New York

Visit us on the Web! www.randomhouse.com/kids
Educators and librarians, for a variety of teaching tools, visit us at
www.randomhouse.com/teachers

Library of Congress Cataloging-in-Publication Data is available upon request.

The text of this book is set in 14-point Garamond.

Book design by Jason Zamajtuk

Printed in the United States of America

May 2004

10 9 8 7 6 5 4 3 2 1

BVG

*This book is dedicated to
Toshiko Yoshida.*

CHAPTER 1

SKEETER GIG. BACK LATE, DON'T WAIT UP. DINNER'S IN
THE FUDGE. LOVE, MOM & DAD

Billy Clikk read the Post-it again.

"*Fridge.* She meant fridge." Crumpling up the yellow square, Billy chucked it at the garbage can and watched it fly in and then bounce out onto the kitchen floor. It was the third time this week he'd come home from school to find his parents gone, leaving him to heat leftovers in the microwave, do his homework, and put himself to bed. At this point they could just leave a note reading THE USUAL and he'd know exactly what it meant.

There was an upside, though: Billy was now free to kick back and watch his favorite TV show, *Truly Twisted.* He dashed into the living room, leaped over the couch, grabbed the remote, and switched on the TV.

Truly Twisted was the one program his parents said he must never, never watch. These guys took extreme sports to a whole new level: they once snuck into a church, climbed up the steeple, and bungee-jumped right into the middle of some guy's wedding. It was pretty awesome.

When Billy got to the channel where *Truly Twisted* was supposed to be airing, though, there was nothing more extreme than some lame college tennis championship. "Oh, come on!" Billy cried. They'd bumped the best show on cable for a couple of scrawny guys knocking a ball back and forth.

Billy shut off the TV and slouched back into the kitchen. He yanked open the "fudge," pulled out a brown paper bag, and peeked inside. Cold chicken curry: carryout from the Delhi Deli, an Indian restaurant down the street. Billy used to like their chicken curry. Back before he'd eaten it once or twice a week, every week, for about three years.

Billy pursed his lips, made a farting sound, and tossed the bag back in the refrigerator. He slammed the door a lot harder than he really needed to and stared at the floor. There, next to his foot, sat the crumpled-up Post-it note.

"Are pest problems getting *you* down?" he said, suddenly doing a superdeep TV-commercial voice. "Then you should pick up that phone and call Jim and Linda Clikk, founders of BUGZ-B-GON, the best extermination service in all of Piffling,

Indiana." He leaned down and picked up the wadded note, and as he straightened up, he added a tone of mystery to his voice. The TV commercial had turned into a piece of investigative journalism. "What makes the Clikks so busy? What drives them to spend their every waking hour on extermination jobs—'skeeter gigs,' as they call them? Is it *really* necessary for them to devote so much of their time and energy to saving total strangers from termites and hornets' nests? Is it just for the money, or is killing bugs some kind of a weird power trip?"

Billy took aim with the Post-it and had another shot at the garbage can. This time the note went in and stayed in.

That's more like it.

Billy changed his posture and pivoted on one foot, transforming himself once again into a reporter.

"And what of Jim and Linda's son, Billy? How does *he* feel about all this?" Billy went on, clutching an imaginary microphone as he strode from the kitchen back to the living room. "Well, let's ask him. Billy, how *do* you feel about all this?"

"You want the truth?" said Billy, switching to his own voice. "I think it stinks. I think it's a lousy way to treat a devoted son who is so bright, well behaved, and good-looking."

Billy drew his eyebrows into an expression of great sympathy: he was the reporter again. "Tell me, Billy, do you think it *bothers* your parents that you have to spend so many evenings at home by yourself? Do you think they feel the least bit *guilty* that you have to eat takeout night after night rather than home-cooked meals? Indeed, do you suppose—as your parents dash madly from one skeeter gig to another—that they even *think* of you *at all*?"

Billy stopped, stood between the couch and the coffee table, and let out a long sigh. He dropped the imaginary microphone and the phony voice along with it.

"I don't know." Billy flopped onto the couch. "Probably not."

It hadn't been so bad the previous year, when Billy's best friend, Nathan Burns, was still living in Piffling. Nathan was the only kid at Piffling Elementary who was as obsessed with extreme sports as Billy was. They used to spend practically every weekend together, mountain-biking the cliffs that led down to the Piffling River, skateboarding across every handrail in town (they both had the scrapes, bruises, and occasional fractures to prove it), and even street luging on their homemade luges, which was apparently outlawed by some city ordinance or another. The only thing Billy and Nathan hadn't tried was sneaking a ride on the brand-new Harley-Davidson Nathan's father had stashed away in the garage.

They would have tried it eventually, for sure. But then Nathan's family moved to Los Angeles for his father's work. There were other kids at Piffling Elementary who were into extreme sports a little. They just weren't willing to risk life and limb the way Nathan was. Billy soon realized that finding a new best friend was going to take a while. In the meantime, it was looking like it would be THE USUAL for many months to come.

Piker, Billy's Scottish terrier, lifted her head from the recliner on the other side of the room, snorted, and went back to sleep.

BACK LATE, DON'T WAIT UP.

Billy had never been able to figure out why so much of his parents' work was done at night. Exterminators didn't normally work at night, did they? Were they trying to catch the bugs snoozing? Kids at school thought he was lucky. "If my parents left *me* alone at night like that," Nelson Skubblemeyer had said just the other day, "I'd be partyin' like nobody's business. I'd be, like, 'Yo, party tonight at my place. . . .' " (Nelson always said the word *party* as if it rhymed with *sauté*: in spite of his name, he'd somehow convinced himself he was the coolest kid in the sixth grade.)

Billy had never thrown a party while his parents were out on a skeeter gig. He wouldn't have been able to get away with it even if he'd tried. There was someone keeping an eye on him.

DRRIIIIIIINGG

Leo Krebs, thought Billy. *Right on schedule.* Billy normally didn't let the phone ring more than twice before answering. But when he was pretty sure it was Leo, the high school sophomore down the street who "looked after" him whenever his parents were gone at night, he had a policy of screening calls.

DRRIIIIIINGG

Billy leaned back into the couch and did his best Leo impersonation: "Dude. Pick up. I know you're there." Doing a good Leo meant breathing a lot of air into your voice and ending every sentence as if it were a question. Like Keanu Reeves, only more so.

DRRIIIIIINGG

Billy's voice had begun to change the previous summer, greatly increasing the range of impersonations he could do (which had been pretty impressive to begin with). "Duu-ude. You're wastin' my time here."

DRRIIIIIINGG

One more ring and the answering machine would kick in.

DRRIIIIIINGG

There was a *plick,* then a *jrrrr,* then: "Your pest problems are at an end . . . ," Jim Clikk's voice said. Billy jumped in and recited the words right along with the answering machine, creating the effect of two Jim Clikks speaking simultaneously. ". . . because you're seconds away from making an appointment with the extermination experts at BUGZ-B-GON. Just leave your name and number after the tone and we'll get back to you as soon as we can."

DWEEEEEP

"Dude." It was Leo, all right. "Pick up. I know you're there."

Billy grabbed the remote off the coffee table and clicked the television on. When dealing with one of Leo's check-in calls, it was essential to have every bit of audiovisual distraction available.

"Duu-ude. You're wastin' my time here."

Billy reached over, grabbed the cordless phone from one of the side tables, and pressed Talk.

"Leonard," he said, knowing how much Leo disliked being called by his full name. Well, at least he *hoped* Leo disliked it. Billy didn't exactly hate Leo, but he wasn't too crazy about him either. Part of it was Leo's *I'm older than you and don't forget it* attitude. Most of it, though, was Billy resenting the whole idea of being baby-sat at all. He was old enough to take care of himself.

"Dude," said Leo in return. He never called Billy anything other than dude. Leo probably called little old ladies dude. "Look, your folks told me they wouldn't be back until, like, midnight or whatever . . ."

Billy was remoting his way through a bunch of cartoon shows. He paused on an old low-budget monster movie.

". . . so I can either come over there and babysit you for a couple hours—which neither of us wants—or just check in again at ten and make sure you're still alive. Not that I want you to be."

"C'mon, Leonard. You don't want anything bad to happen to me. You'd be out twenty bucks a week."

Normally Billy would have come up with a better verbal jab than the twenty bucks line, but he was devoting most of his attention to the image on the television screen: an enormous creature with lobster claws going to great lengths to stomp his way into a cheap imitation of Disneyland. There didn't seem to be any special reason why. Maybe he'd run out of office buildings and power stations to wreck.

"All right, dude. Ten o'clock it is. Pick up the phone next time, will ya?"

"Okay, Leonard. And hey: tell your skater buddies to learn some new moves. My gramma can do better kickflips than that."

Billy shut off the phone with great relief. He knew that the money his parents paid Leo involved him physically being inside the Clikk home. Periodically Leo would skip the phone call and just arrive at the front door. On these occasions he always left behind some very clear proof that he'd been there—doodles on a notepad, a half-finished bottle of Gatorade—apparently thinking a bit of Leo-was-here evidence every once in a while would be enough to convince Billy's parents they weren't completely wasting their twenty dollars.

Doodles on notepads. Bottles of Gatorade. Billy noticed stuff like that: details. He'd always had a knack for it, even when he was just a kindergartner. If the dark blue crayon in Crayola's big box went from being called cerulean one year to cornflower the next, Billy knew about it and had a preference. And it wasn't just kid stuff. If Billy got even half a second's glance under the hood of a Hummer H2, he could tell which parts were new, which were old, and which parts the shady repairman had used strictly to skim money off the bill.

The lobster creature had reached the roller-coaster mountain in the middle of the amusement park and was tearing apart its papier-mâché walls. Sweaty actors with loosened neckties pointed and screamed convincingly.

Man. This is one stupid movie. If I were fighting a monster like that, I'd just pull the zipper on his back, stick my head inside, and tell him to get a better costume.

Billy punched the remote and jumped from channel 63 to 64. The Shopping Network: two middle-aged women going nuts over a very ugly piece of jewelry. Punch, punch, punch, punch: 65, 66, 67, 68. Boring, boring, boring, and boring. He was just about to shut the television off.

Huh?

That guy on TV.

That guy looked an *awful* lot like his dad.

Billy sat up and leaned halfway over the coffee table, staring with all his might. Piker sat up too.

The TV screen was filled with unsteady handheld video: some kind of ticker-tape parade. Street signs in a foreign language, early-morning sunlight. Dark-haired people with open-necked shirts, shouting, cheering. And there, in a big convertible sailing slowly through the crowds . . .

That's Dad!

No, it can't be.

Billy pressed the VCR button on the remote and then hit Record.

Bee-beep, bee-beep, bee-beep

"No tape!" Billy jumped off the couch, leaped over the coffee table, and fumbled for a blank videotape from the shelf under the TV, all the while keeping his eyes glued to the screen. Piker jumped down from the chair and began whining loudly.

"That can't be him," said Billy. "It's impossible."

Billy's heart was beating faster. He tore the cellophane off the videotape and crammed it into the VCR as quickly as he could. He punched the Record button and sat down on the coffee table to continue watching the program.

"That's not Dad. It just . . . can't be. This stuff was obviously shot in a foreign country. Dad never goes to other countries. Except, like, Canada."

But the man had the same face as Billy's father: the wide forehead, the slightly grayed wavy hair, the enormous protruding jaw. There was a woman seated next to him. It was hard to tell because she was wearing a wide-brimmed hat, but that was . . . Billy's mom, wasn't it? She had the same perky nose, the same thin-lipped mouth, and—from what he could see, anyway—was wearing the exact same style of thick-rimmed glasses.

No. Way.

Billy was now leaning so far forward that his face was no more than ten inches from the TV screen. He noticed something about the trees and buildings in the video: everything was dripping with some kind of thick, purplish liquid. As if kids had gone on a rampage with giant purple-yolked eggs.

What the heck is that stuff?

Piker barked once loudly.

A woman's voice accompanied the video, no doubt providing valuable information, but none of it was in English. A small icon in the lower right-hand corner of the TV screen confirmed what Billy already suspected: this was the International Channel, that weird cable station that went from Middle Eastern movies to Korean soap operas to Mexican news programs every half hour or so.

Billy trained his eyes on the pixelated faces before him. The camera zoomed in, went drastically out of focus, refocused on a palm tree, then finally brought the faces into some degree of detail. It *was* them. There could be no mistaking it. These were the same two people he'd eaten breakfast with, gone to monster truck shows with, and opened presents with every Christmas morning for the last twelve years.

The footage cut abruptly to a woman behind a desk reading the news. She had deeply tanned skin and almond-shaped eyes. Though she had yet to say a single word in English, Billy could tell by the way she paused and shuffled the papers in front of her that she was switching from one news story to another.

Billy was now off the coffee table and on his feet. He pressed Rewind and watched the video again. And again. And again. He memorized the details: the fruits in the market off to the side of the road (there were papayas, mangos, and bananas by the truckload), the make of the convertible (it was a black 1965 Lincoln Continental, in near-perfect condition), the footwear of the people in the crowd (sandals, one and all). He tried to decipher the words on street signs. One looked like it said DELA ROSA, another DELA COSTA.

This stuff was definitely *shot in a foreign country. My parents . . . are . . . in a foreign country.*

Billy rewound the tape for yet another viewing.

At least they have *been pretty recently, or else why would this be on a news show? It's morning where they are, nighttime here. This isn't just another country. They're on the other side of the freakin' planet here.*

SKEETER GIG. BACK LATE, DON'T WAIT UP.

Billy felt his knees buckle slightly, as if they were straining under the weight of not just his body but something else. Something heavier. Something much, much heavier.

"Skeeter gig?" said Billy. "*Skeeter* gig?"

A shiver ran down his spine and he swallowed hard.

"My parents didn't go on any skeeter gig. They . . . they *snuck off* somewhere . . . without *telling* me.

"Mom and Dad don't do stuff like this. It's, like, a major event with them when they cross the state line into Illinois. And now they're on the other side of the world? This is just *way* too weird to even be possible."

Then it hit him: he'd been tricked.

"Mom and Dad lied to me."

They were words he'd never had to say before.

CHAPTER 2

Billy was pacing madly around the living room, flipping through the cable guide. Piker followed along behind him.

When he got to the page he needed, he ran his finger down until it landed on the rectangle that corresponded with the channel and time slot he'd been watching:

FILIPINO NEWS DAILY

"The Philippines? That's, like, twelve hours ahead of central time, so . . . it *was* live: morning there, nighttime here.

That footage was shot in the Philippines. Mom and Dad went to the Philippines!

"But why? What would they do that for?"

His mind was racing, trying to come up with explanations, possibilities.

Maybe they needed a special kind of insecticide. Something you can't get anywhere but the Philippines.

Signs in foreign languages. Confetti. *His parents.*

"Maybe they got called to the Philippines for a skeeter gig. Maybe Mom and Dad are, like, Philippine bug experts or something."

His heart was pounding at an incredible rate. He felt sweaty all of a sudden, feverish. Piker trotted after him as he marched back into the kitchen, stopped in front of the refrigerator, opened it, and pulled out the brown bag.

Okay. Say they're Philippine bug experts. When are they going to come back? What's gonna happen *when they come back?*

Without thinking about it too much he opened the bag, pulled out the container inside, got a spoon, and started eating the ice-cold chicken curry. He didn't sit down.

And what's with the confetti? Why would people in the Philippines be treating my parents like heroes?

Maybe Mom and Dad helped them get rid of some really nasty bugs, and the locals were so happy they decided to celebrate.

Or maybe this has nothing to do with bugs. Maybe they're just on vacation.

It was one thing to have parents who were never at home

because they were out hunting termites. It was quite another if they were never at home because they were vacationing without him in a foreign country, laughing it up in the middle of some big freaky parade.

The cold chicken curry tasted awful. He shoveled it into his mouth.

"Maybe it *wasn't* them. Maybe it was . . . a couple of people who . . . by an amazing coincidence . . . look exactly like them . . . and live in the Philippines."

The jaw. The big toothy grin. The little mole just to the side of his left nostril. That *was* his father. He was sure of it.

"Okay."

Billy inhaled.

He exhaled, slowly.

"All right." He began to address his comments to Piker, as if he were a lawyer and she were in the jury box. "Let's say that was them. They work hard. They needed a vacation, so they went to the Philippines . . ."

He was done with the chicken curry. It left a terrible taste in his mouth. He licked the spoon.

". . . and ended up in a parade, um, as the guests of honor. That's not so weird. That probably happens a lot."

That has probably never happened in the history of mankind.

"Okay. What if . . . I'm just saying *what if,* now . . . what if this isn't a one-time-only deal? What if *every time* they've told me they were going on a skeeter gig they were . . . secretly . . . going to the Philippines? Or even other countries, who knows where?" His stomach tightened as he said the words.

"What if they have this weird . . . whole other *life* . . . that they haven't been telling me about?" His stomach tightened even more.

I can't believe they'd pull this stuff on me. It's like they don't even care *about me.*

"Look, stay calm. The first thing you need to do is find out what they're up to. Get more info."

They couldn't pull something like this off without prepping for it first. There's gotta be stuff lying around here that'll tell me what they're up to.

He took the stairs three at a time up to his parents' bedroom. Piker was with him every step of the way.

He surveyed the room. It was just the same as it had always been: the clunky bed with tree trunks for legs that looked as if it had been hauled back from a hunting lodge, the totally mismatched dressers (one cherry, the other unvarnished pine), the messy stacks of pack-rat junk that filled his mother's walk-in closet. He'd seen it all a thousand times before. But now every nook and cranny seemed to be a potential source of incriminating evidence. He went to his mother's bedside table, yanked open the drawer, and rifled through its contents. There were hair bands, nail files, a tube of hand cream . . . nothing suspicious. He shut the drawer and glanced at the stack of romance novels on top of the table: thick paperbacks with pink-and-purple covers featuring bare-chested longhaired men kissing women with hair of about the same length.

"Come on. Mom reads *romance novels*. She's not the secret vacation type."

He picked one up and flipped through the pages. "I don't get it. My parents aren't cool enough to sneak off to the Philippines. And even if they were, it's not like they have loads of cash for this. . . ."

His eyes zeroed in on the pages of the book. The words were in a foreign language. Well, *some* of them were. Parts of it were in English.

He fumbled back to the title page, where, according to the cover, he should find the words *Whisper of the Gypsies: A Tale of Forbidden Passion by Deedee Strauss*. He found instead:

Teach Yourself Tagalog!
Speak Like a Native Filipino in Less Than Ten Minutes a Day

He drew the book up to his eyes and took a very close look at the spine. The shiny purple cover had been removed from a romance novel, neatly trimmed, and pasted over the cover of this book, which definitely had *nothing* to do with Gypsies.

Billy was starting to feel angry now. His mom and dad had been sneaking around like a couple of secret agents for who knew how long. This was some seriously freaky stuff they were pulling on him.

Piker whined and rumbled out of the room. Seconds later he heard her paws flailing against the door to the backyard. Normally whenever Piker did this Billy would jump up and run to let her out.

Not tonight.

He swept the remaining romance novels off the table with both hands, sat down on his parents' bed, and flipped quickly from one title page to the next:

Conversational Finnish Made Easy
Instant Portuguese
So You Want to Speak Swahili?

There wasn't a single *real* romance novel in the stack.

Billy's throat was now very, very dry, and he felt a headache coming on. He dumped all the books back on the bedside table, making no attempt to put them back the way they'd been.

It's not just the Philippines. They've been going all over the place: Europe! Africa!

"This . . . is unreal."

They've been tricking me. Lying to me! They've probably been flying off to another country every other day, all my life.

He was dumbstruck and angry and scared and hurt all at once. He felt as if the whole world had been ripped away from him and replaced with some weird episode of *The Twilight Zone*: a landscape that kept shifting and changing every time he turned his head.

I've gotta stay calm. Gotta deal with this. Just deal with it.

He looked around the room. He needed more clues, more pieces of the puzzle. If he gathered enough of them, he could figure out what was going on.

He spent the next half hour going through his parents' stuff: their drawers, their closets, their clothing, even their toiletries. But he found nothing more unusual than an old denim jacket in his father's closet emblazoned with the words STUD FOR HIRE.

Ridiculous? Yes.

An important clue? Man, I hope not.

He looked under the bed: nothing.

He rifled through his mother's jewelry case: nothing.

He even checked behind paintings on the wall for a hidden safe: nothing.

There's got to be someplace I haven't checked.

He took one last look around the room, his eyes jumping from object to object, until . . .

The trash can!

Billy dashed to the plastic wastepaper basket on his father's side of the bed, dropped to his knees, and began digging through it.

He removed an orange rind and tossed it on the floor. Next came an empty box of Kleenex and a folded newspaper (the *Piffling Herald,* though something covered with Egyptian hieroglyphics wouldn't have entirely surprised him at this point). "I can*not* believe they've been keeping all this stuff secret from me. Secret travel, secret languages, secret—"

Receipts.

Billy was sifting through a handful of them: blue ink on white paper, the scraps that get printed out and stuffed into your hand pretty much anywhere you buy anything. These receipts, though, were *not* from stores in Piffling. One looked as if it was in Arabic, another in Chinese.

His heart was really starting to pound like crazy now.

Digging deeper, he found a handwritten receipt from a store called the Outpost in Nome, Alaska. The neat cursive words were unmistakable:

Sled ($195.00 per day for three days).................. *$585.00*

Dog team (8 dogs at $95.00 per dog per day)...... *$2,280.00*

Stapled to this receipt was another, stained with dark brown blotches. Written on it, in a messy ballpoint scrawl, he read:

Salmon heads, 250 lbs.................... $112.83

Salmon heads? *Salmon heads?* Two hundred and fifty *pounds* of them?

Billy broke into a cold sweat. He flipped back to the first receipt and checked the date.

No way. This was just last week, when Dad was attending an extermination seminar in Cleveland.

"Dad wasn't in Cleveland last week. He was in *Alaska*. He spent a hundred and twelve dollars and, and . . ."

He flipped back to the other receipt.

". . . and eighty-three cents. He spent it . . . on salmon heads."

Why would Dad buy so many salmon heads? A fishing expedition? Walrus hunting? That's not even legal. Don't tell me my goofball dad is an outlaw. I just can't buy that.

Billy made up his mind then and there. He was going to figure this thing out. He didn't care if it took all night or if he had to
tear the house apart, he was going to get to the bottom of this. And
when his parents got home, he'd throw it all right in their faces.

Piker tore back into the room, a leash clenched in her
teeth, whining her very loudest now-now-*right*-now whine.

"Sorry, Pike. Pee on the living room carpet if you have to,
I'm busy." Billy upended the garbage can and dumped its entire
contents. Piker groaned.

A few walnut shells twirled out of the mess, slid across the hardwood floor, and glided under Dad's dresser.

TWING

"Twing?" Billy peered into the shadowy slit between the bottom of the dresser and the floor. One of the walnut shells had hit something underneath the dresser and made a *twing*ing sound.

Walnut shells don't make twinging sounds underneath dressers.

Billy got down on his hands and knees.

Not unless they hit something . . . twingworthy.

He reached one hand under the dresser. First he found the walnut shells. He tossed them aside, reached farther back, and laid his fingers on . . . something. It was small, cold, and metallic. He pulled it out into the light.

It was his father's business card case: silver, spotless, smooth as a mirror. Billy had never been allowed to touch it. His father must have knocked it off the top of the dresser by accident. He'd probably been going crazy looking for it.

Billy turned the shimmering case over in his hands. It had always struck him as odd that an exterminator would have such a fancy-shmancy business card case. But now it struck him as more than odd. It was suspicious, almost sinister.

This thing is one of the secrets. One of the big ones.

Billy popped it open and took out one of the cards:

A thought flashed into Billy's head: a revelation so startling—and so undeniable—that it seemed to hit him physically, like a punch in the gut.

BUGZ-B-GON is a lie. There is no BUGZ-B-GON. My parents aren't exterminators. They're . . .

Billy crushed the card in his fist and threw it across the room.

. . . something else.

Piker had a strange look in her eyes. As if she knew what he was thinking and wanted to stop him from thinking it.

All these years I thought they were working late to build up the business . . . it was all just a scam. There is no business. Or if there is, it has nothing to do with bugs.

Billy turned the case over one more time and saw something he'd missed the first time around, the sort of detail he'd been training himself to see for years: a tiny button on one side of the case, small as a pimple. He pushed it. There was a soft mechanical whirr as a business card slid out from the bottom of the case, like a high-tech slice of toast. The card was made of steel and had letters engraved on it. They read:

AFMEC

JIM AND LINDA CLIKK
SENIOR AGENTS SINCE 1988
NORTH AMERICAN DIVISION, SECTOR FOUR

1-800-CREATCH

"AFMEC?"

Senior Agents. They're members of some weird secret society.

"North American Division? Sector Four? Jeez, whatever it is, it's global. It's some sort of secret international organization."

Are they spies? Crime fighters? Criminals?

"1-800-CREATCH."

Piker whimpered.

"All right, that does it. Enough digging around this stupid house already. I'm calling this number."

Billy pointed a finger at Piker. "You wanna know what AFMEC is?"

Piker groaned as if it were the very last thing on earth she wanted to know.

"Well, *I* do. And I'm about to find out."

Billy went to the phone.

CHAPTER 3

Billy raised the receiver to his ear and prepared to dial the number.

"Wait." He put the phone back in its catch. "Can't make this call cold. Gotta get myself ready first."

Piker seemed to mellow out as soon as Billy put the phone down.

"What's the deal, Piker?" asked Billy as he ran to his bedroom. "Don't have to go anymore?"

Billy jumped over the piles of stuff that covered his bedroom floor—mud-spattered knee pads, neon-striped skateboards, fallen rock-climbing posters—and fired up his computer: a Macintosh, one of the newest models. Billy's parents had nixed the idea of buying a new television, but they were extremely cool when it came to computers. "It's educational," his dad always said. "That's different." Billy was on his third brand-new computer.

"Come on. Warm up already."

As soon as he was able to log on he Googled the word *AFMEC*. Scanning the list of results, he came up with only three possibilities. First was something called the Agriculture and Fisheries Mechanization Committee, which was located—bingo!—in the Philippines. Still, it didn't look like a big enough organization to account for all the globe-trotting his parents had been up to.

"I don't know. Maybe it's just a front or something."

Next was the U.S. Air Force Media Center. It certainly sounded more impressive than the fisheries committee, but it didn't appear to be anything more than a tiny division of the military—and in any case, its activities were limited to duplicating videocassettes and cataloging stock footage of jets taking off and landing.

"Naw. They wouldn't bother being so sneaky about boring stuff like this."

Finally came Al's Fancy Mayonnaise and Eggnog Company. This one Billy rejected almost immediately, but not before wondering why on earth a guy would go into the business of selling both eggnog and mayonnaise. "That's just gross. I'm sorry."

Billy spent about a half hour chasing down every lead he could think of based on the words he'd seen on the card: *North*

American Division, Sector Four, even the 1-800-CREATCH phone number. There were loads of results for the first two—none of them related to AFMEC, so far as he could tell—and no results whatsoever for the toll-free number.

Whoever gets these cards must be under strict orders not to put the number on the Web. Like, under punishment of death or something.

After a few more searches for anything related to the news story he'd seen (he found nothing), the Outpost in Nome (he found an extremely lame Web page), and even the author of *So You Want to Speak Swahili?* (he found way more than he had any intention of reading), Billy realized he'd reached the end of what the Internet could teach him about all this.

"All right. Time to make the call."

As Billy picked up the telephone next to his computer, Piker—who had been waiting politely outside the door—seemed to suddenly rediscover her need to pee.

"Look, I swear, Pike. I won't get mad if you do it on the carpet. Knock yourself out."

Piker groaned and began pacing.

Deet . . . deet-deet-deet . . .

"One eight hundred," said Billy as he pressed the numbers.

His plan was simple: get hold of someone at this AFMEC place and pry as much information out of the person as he could.

Deet . . . deet . . . deet-deet . . .

"C . . . R . . . E, A . . ."

Judging by how secretive AFMEC insiders were, he knew that anyone he spoke to there would have been told not to give out information to strangers. Least of all strangers who sounded like twelve-year-old boys.

Deet . . . deet . . . deet.

". . . T . . . C . . . H."

So he would have to do an impersonation. Probably the most important impersonation of his life. Billy Clikk was going to impersonate Jim Clikk.

Billy was good at imitating his father's voice. He'd been working on it for years, mainly just to make jokes. But now was not a time for jokes. Now it was time for the real thing: a Jim Clikk imitation so convincing even the people he worked for would be fooled.

Can I pull this off?

Sure. I can do it. Just gotta stay calm.

After one or two rings a recorded message came on:

"Welcome to AFMEC," said a man's voice, deep and far less cheerful-sounding than your average recorded message. It was some sort of European accent: Billy immediately knew that AFMEC was neither an air force media center nor a Filipino fisheries committee.

"Please hold while our computers register your location. . . ."

Billy swallowed hard. Whoever he was calling would know exactly where he was. That was pretty scary. No, that was *extremely* scary.

For a moment Billy considered hanging up, but curiosity won out. He held the line.

A different recorded voice came on—a woman's, slightly more cheerful-sounding—and began to list options:

"If this is a creatch-related emergency, please press *zero, pound* now."

Creatch, thought Billy. *That's the key word here. Gotta find out what it means.*

He grabbed a pencil and started taking notes.

"If you would like to report a creatch sighting, press *one* now."

Piker was at Billy's feet, wearing a very undoglike expression. She looked as if she were in very serious trouble and were trying to think of a way out.

"If you are a government official inquiring about a pending creatch-control treaty with AFMEC, please press *two*, followed by your country code, now."

Billy wrote down every word, but what he really needed was an option that went something like this: "If you have recently discovered that your parents are not who they say they are and are trying to figure out what the heck it is they actually *do* for a living . . ."

His fears began to resurface, telling him to put the phone down and forget the whole thing. But he needed answers. What was AFMEC? Why were his parents going everywhere from the Philippines to Finland to Nome? What did people who worked for AFMEC do? And why did they need enormous quantities of salmon heads to do it?

"If you are a demi-creatch or a creatch informant wishing to apply for AFMEC protection, please press *three* now."

Piker picked up the leash with her teeth in a final attempt to interest Billy in a walk around the block. Billy turned away and looked out the window. The sun had sunk into the woods at the far end of Dullard Road, leaving the sky pinkish gray and empty, apart from a single trail of exhaust coming from an airplane he couldn't see.

"If you are an AFMEC agent calling to get in touch with AFMEC headquarters, please hang up and call again using your viddy-fone."

There was a very long silence. Billy sensed that this was the last option, and with great disappointment—but also a certain amount of relief—he prepared to follow its advice: the hanging up part, anyway.

But then there was a crackle and the voice continued.

"If you are an AFMEC agent and have misplaced or damaged your viddy-fone, please stay on the line."

A click. A burst of static. Then a bit of soft dentist-office music, almost inaudible: about fifty violins playing the theme from a movie that must have been extremely long and sappy.

Piker leaped up and began pawing at Billy's legs.

"Down!" Billy twisted his body as he tried to get away from her. *"Doowww—"*

"Mr. Clikk?"

The music had stopped. A man's voice was on the line.

"Mr. Clikk?"

Piker looked on in horror. Billy held the phone with both hands and swallowed again.

"Jim Clikk? Is that you?"

Show time.

"Yeah," Billy said now as Piker gave up and dropped to the floor. "Yeah, uh . . . this is, uh, Jim Clikk here, that's right." He winced, realizing he should have just left it at the *yeah.*

"You all right, Jim? You sound funny."

Billy coughed loudly. A big, showy Broadway cough. "Got a cold. Uh . . . something I picked up in the Philippines . . ."

"So what's the deal, Jim?" the man said after a moment, apparently taking this as an acceptable explanation. "Can't find your viddy-fone?"

"Yeah. Sorry."

"I'll have HQ send out a new one right away."

"Thanks."

"So how'd that creatch op turn out? I hear you ended up on the local news, Jim. Just can't resist being the center of attention, can you?" The man followed this with a knowing chuckle. Billy tried to laugh appropriately.

"Better watch out. You know how HQ feels about the media. Remember François Guilliarde? Did an interview with *Le Monde* and they demoted him to cleanup operations, poor guy."

Billy felt it had been too long since he'd said something. So he said, "Right."

"Anything else I can do for you, Jim?"

Stay calm. Talk the way Dad would.

"Yeah, uh, any word on what my next . . . assignment is?"

"Assignment?" A trace of suspicion had crept into the man's voice. "What, you mean your next creatch op?"

"Yeah, that's right. Next creatch op." Billy was sweating. The voice part was going well, but he had to watch the vocabulary.

"Well, no, Jim," said the man. "You know I don't have access to that kind of info. No one tells me what's happening until it's already happening."

Okay. That's going nowhere.

"Oh, right, of course. Um, say, I've got this receipt here . . . uh, for salmon heads I bought in Nome, Alaska, a couple weeks back. . . ."

"Yeah?" Billy heard computer keys clacking away. "What about it?"

"Well, for my records, uh . . . I'm just hoping you can remind me of the, uh, creatch op that those salmon heads were, were . . . related to."

A pause.

"You mean you . . . don't remember?"

He's on to you. Play it off.

"Course I remember! Sure. It's just with, uh, all the different creatch ops we've been handling, you know . . . it's hard to . . . keep them all straight."

There was a very long pause. Billy sensed that something was wrong. Terribly, terribly wrong.

"Who is this?"

Billy froze. His cover was blown. Completely.

He slammed the phone down. He was breathing hard and dripping with sweat.

Who is this? The words echoed in Billy's head.

Man oh man. I blew it. I'm in serious trouble now. Big time.

Piker was glaring at him. Dogs aren't capable of saying things like "Look what you've gone and done, you fool." Still, seeing the expression on Piker's face, Billy half expected her to say something along those lines.

"Look, I *had* to make that call," Billy said, justifying his actions to a dog. "I found out some valuable information: that, that . . . that Mom and Dad were in the Philippines on some sort of mission or something called a creatch op. That people who do these creatch ops aren't supposed to allow themselves to be on TV or in the newspapers. That's all, you know, valuable information."

Piker looked unconvinced.

Who is this?

All the information in the world, valuable or not, couldn't have made up for the awful thought that had crept into Billy's head as soon as he slammed that phone down. It was the thought that he'd crossed a line. A line he shouldn't have crossed. As if he had opened a door marked AUTHORIZED PERSONNEL ONLY and an alarm had gone off. Not an alarm he could hear. An alarm someone *else* could hear. Somewhere far away.

A terrible panic set in. The Billy from a moment ago—the one who had decided he was going to get to the bottom of this if it took all night—was gone. He had been replaced by a Billy who felt that, on the whole, getting halfway to the bottom of it was such an unpleasant experience that maybe going back up to the top wouldn't be such a bad idea.

But Billy knew it was too late to reverse course. He wasn't sure when his parents would be back. Judging from experience, he guessed he still had a few more hours to go: they usually came back from their skeeter gigs sometime between midnight and dawn. But what to do until then? He had to keep himself busy or his head would explode.

I'll just do the usual stuff. The nightly routine. It'll calm me down, get me breathing normally again.

So Billy did his English homework.

Popped some popcorn.

Ate it.

Brushed his teeth.

Climbed into bed.

Turned out the lights.

And closed his eyes.

He didn't go to sleep, though. The way he was feeling, he wondered if he'd ever be able to sleep again.

Something's going to happen, he thought. *I'm going to get in trouble for that phone call. That guy on the phone will tell Mom and Dad what I did. Then what? Gotta have a plan. A plan for what I'll do when they come home . . .*

Billy tried to imagine what was going to happen to him as a result of the phone call. He came up with a number of scenarios, all of which involved people being angry at him, and some of which involved the local police coming to the front door. None of the scenarios he came up with involved a five-member creach containment squadron smashing through his bedroom window at 10:06 P.M.

That, however, was exactly what happened.

CHAPTER 4

Glass flew everywhere. Billy jumped, sitting straight up in bed, and briefly considered (but quickly rejected) the possibility that this was nothing more than a curry-induced hallucination.

There in the darkness, tinted blue by the moonlight coming through the window, were five gray-suited figures: four men, one woman, each wearing a pair of wraparound sunglasses. They were all down on one knee, surrounding Billy's bed in a neat semicircle, arms extended, with strange pear-shaped pistols

aimed squarely at Billy's head. Two or three of them were panting quietly.

"Don't move," said one, a middle-aged man with a neatly trimmed mustache. "We are placing you under arrest," he continued, "for violations of AFMEC code 574, section six, paragraph two: impersonating an AFMEC member with the intent to subvert AFMEC operations."

I did cross a line, thought Billy. *A very, very, very big line.* He wanted to ask a question but under the circumstances assumed he needed to request permission to do so. He raised his hand.

The mustached man removed his sunglasses. He had dark circles under his eyes, as if he hadn't slept for a few days.

"Yes?" the mustached man said. "What is it?"

"Am I in any less trouble if my parents are members of . . . AFMEC?"

The man frowned. "I'm sure they'll take that into consideration, Billy. First we have to make sure you're not a cr—" He stopped himself. "We need to check you out a little first. Freud," he said to one of the others. "Will you do the honors?"

"Certainly, Mr. Twain."

Freud? Twain? As in Sigmund Freud and Mark Twain?

Billy's eyes darted back and forth between the two men.

Code names. They've gotta be.

The man called Freud moved quickly to Billy's side and swept the blanket off the bed in one fluid movement. Billy jumped back, knocking his head soundly against the wall. His heart was beating like mad.

What's he going to do to me?

Freud had a small machine about the size and shape of a video camera, which he held just in front of Billy's face. It buzzed and beeped and gave off a weird odor of electrodes and circuits: the smell of a new appliance, fresh from the store. Two of the men and the woman moved closer to the bed, their pear pistols at near point-blank range.

Billy was terrified. He didn't know what the machine was for, but it was now producing a series of whirring, grinding noises that made him think it could cause him serious harm.

"Stick out your tongue," said Freud.

"What?"

"*Now.* Stick out your tongue." Freud had an odd voice. It hissed a little, like an old phonograph.

He's going to cut off my tongue. It's punishment for making that phone call!

"I'm not going to hurt you. Just . . . do as you are told."

"No," said Billy. "I don't know you people. You crash through my window. You point weird weapons at me. And now you stick a machine in front of my face and think I'm going to trust you? No way, man. No way."

Freud shot Twain a quizzical glance.

"Look, Billy," said Twain. "You're . . ." He paused and exhaled, long and slow. "You're in way over your head here. If you don't cooperate, you're only going to make things worse for yourself. A *lot* worse."

Billy examined Twain's face. The squinty eyes, the thin mustache. It wasn't the sort of face Billy wanted to trust. Still, what Twain said was true enough. Billy *was* in way over his head. And like it or not, these people seemed to be completely in charge, at least for the time being.

"Now," said Twain, "are you going to stick out your tongue or not?"

Billy swallowed hard.

Gotta cooperate. There's no other choice right now.

He opened his mouth and stuck out his tongue.

Freud raised the machine until it was just a few inches from Billy's tongue, then pushed one of the buttons.

Doors popped open.

klik

    chik

       tzzzz

Things moved quickly just below Billy's field of vision. He felt, but did not see, something clamp onto his tongue, draw it out as far as it would go, and hold it in place. There was a brief stabbing sensation near the tip of his tongue: painful, but not excruciating. Billy tried to say "Ouch" but it came out as "Ahhhth."

The machine let go of Billy's tongue, causing it to snap back into his mouth. There were three *beeps,* three *kliks,* and one loud *boop.* After a moment Freud's face was bathed with blue light from a small video screen on his side of the machine.

"He's a sape," said Freud. "Twelve years old. Son of . . . Jim and Linda. Yes. He checks out."

All five of Billy's captors breathed a sigh. Three of them stood up and stretched their arms, cracked their necks. They all took off their sunglasses. Billy noticed with horror that one of them—the woman—had enormous eyes, at least twice as large as normal.

Where's Mom and Dad? I can't believe they'd leave me alone with these freaks.

"Billy, Billy, Billy," said Twain, pacing like a schoolteacher at the front of a classroom. "You're lucky we were the squadron assigned to you. Some guys are really trigger-happy. You could have been comalized. Or worse."

Billy was furious. Here he was going through the most nightmarish evening of his entire life and this guy was telling him he was lucky.

Who do these people think they are? I ought to demand an apology. And a nice long explanation while we're at it.

He was furious. But he was also scared. He breathed deeply, trying to calm himself down.

Better not push my luck. Who knows what these guys'll do to me if I make them angry? Mom and Dad will come home like they always do—they've got to eventually—and when they do I'll be safe. Safer than I am right now, anyway.

Billy decided to settle for just one more question.

"Look," he said, "the machine says I'm okay. So I'm not in trouble anymore, right?"

"Oh, you're in trouble," said Twain. "Big trouble. And you're not the only one." He turned his head and called in a loud voice, "Orzamo! Get in here!"

The door to Billy's bedroom creaked open and in came Piker: head down, tail between her legs.

Twain talked to the dog as if he were reprimanding a secretary. "What were you doing while he was on the phone? Where *were* you?"

The dog lowered her head farther.

"What are you here for? I mean, come on, Orzamo. You've got a job. One simple job: to prevent things like this from happening."

Billy's head was spinning. This man was calling Piker by a different name. Talking about her having a job. He was *talking* to her, and she was *listening* to him.

Billy stared at Piker, and suddenly his dog was not his dog anymore.

She's in on it. Piker's . . . one of them!

But she's a dog.

Have they been messing with her head somehow?

"I don't know, Orzamo," continued Twain. "This is sloppy. Very sloppy. I expect more of you, and so does HQ."

Billy was shaking. He'd seen some pretty weird things so far, but *this* just didn't seem possible.

No, no, no. There are explanations for all of this. Mom and Dad are going to explain everything. I just gotta cool down and stay in control till they—

DRIIIIIIING

All eyes turned to the phone. Then they turned to Twain. He was deep in thought and had obviously not expected this.

It's Mom and Dad, thought Billy. *They're going to save me from these people.*

DRIIIIIIING

"Answer the phone, Billy," said Twain. "But remember: We're not here." He pointed to all the other gray-suited figures in the room. "As far as the person on the other end of that line is concerned, we don't even exist."

DRIIIIIIING

Billy grabbed the telephone and drew it to his ear.

"Hello?"

"Dude."

Leo!

"You picked up. I like that. Let's make a habit of it."

Billy glanced at Twain, who raised a finger, signaling him not to try any funny stuff.

"Hi, Leo," said Billy, finding himself in the unusual position of doing an impersonation of himself—his calm, everyday, un-freaked-out self. "What's up?"

"Dude, you called me Leo. What's gotten into you? You must be having an excellent evening over there."

Billy swallowed and said nothing.

"All right, dude. You're alive. My work is done."

"Bye, Leo."

"Later."

Billy hung up the phone. *Leo's not in on it,* he thought. *Or else he's a very, very good actor.*

"Well done, Billy," said Twain. "See how smoothly things can go when you cooperate?"

Billy glanced at his shattered bedroom window. *Yeah. Real smooth.*

Twain smiled in a way that creeped Billy out. *Do my parents and this guy really work for the same organization?*

There was a piercing electronic tone:

TEEP

Twain reached into his pocket and pulled out a silver rectangle identical to Jim Clikk's business card case. He opened it like a laptop computer. Billy could see that there was a tiny video screen on the inside of the lid.

So that's *what a viddy-fone is.*

"Yes?" said Twain.

There was a high-pitched voice, too quiet for Billy to hear clearly.

"I see." Twain frowned. More of the tinny voice. "But we're already *here.* Why don't *we* just bring him in and—"

The voice cut him off. Twain exhaled loudly through his nose.

"All right. All right."

The voice said one or two more words. There was a staticky pop and Twain clicked the silver case shut. He turned to the others.

"We're being called off the job. They're going to let Jim and Linda handle it." Two of the men groaned their disapproval.

Billy sighed his relief. *They're putting Mom and Dad in charge? That I can deal with. At least I hope I can. It's like I don't even know them anymore. But they've gotta be cooler than Twain and his goon squad.*

"Come on," said Twain, returning to the window. "Back to the transport."

Billy's heart rate began to slow back down as the five figures left his bedroom, stepped through his shattered window, and climbed a rope ladder up and out of sight.

Twain was the last one to go. He turned to Billy before he left.

"Get dressed, Billy. Go down to the living room and wait. Your parents will be back soon. They're going to take care of all this." He jabbed a finger to make his final point. "You *are* in trouble. Don't forget that."

A moment later he was gone.

Billy leaped out of bed, ran to the window, and stuck his head out. He looked up just in time to see the rope ladder shoot over the edge of the roof and disappear. Seconds later a brief flash of bright green light filled the air, illuminating the leaves of nearby trees and eliciting several loud yelps from a dog across the street. This was followed by a whooshing sound, which grew quieter and quieter, then ceased altogether. Whatever the "transport" was, it was gone now, taking the five gray-suited figures along with it.

Billy stayed there a moment longer, staring out at the trees and rooftops he'd seen from that window all his life. He sensed that his whole world was about to change. That in fact it had already changed, and would never, ever go back to being the way it had been before.

CHAPTER 5

Billy was in the living room.

He was sitting on the couch in a way he had never sat on it before: legs directly in front of him, feet flat on the floor. His back was unnaturally straight and resting against nothing but the air behind it. He was looking at the television, or perhaps at a point in space somewhere on the other side of the television, or even on the other side of town. If he *was* looking at the television, he certainly wasn't seeing much, since the television wasn't switched on.

"Arzamo," he said. It was the first thing he'd said in several minutes. "No. No, it was *Orzamo*, wasn't it?"

He finally tore his eyes away from whatever they'd been looking at and turned them in the direction of his dog. She was sitting in her usual spot: the recliner on the other side of the room. She looked extremely anxious, as if she were getting ready to be punished.

"Orzamo," Billy said again, being careful to put the stress on the *Or*, just as Twain had. "Is that your *real* name?" Piker whimpered in a way that didn't really answer the question.

She understands English. On some basic level she actually understands *what I'm saying. These AFMEC people have probably been beefing up her intelligence with chemicals or genetic engineering or something.*

A silence followed during which neither of them did anything but sit and breathe. The air was heavy with the smell of microwaved popcorn.

Billy's thoughts turned back to his parents. The earlier mix of shock and dismay and hurt had simmered down into a thick bubbly stew of anger.

He looked around the room. All the things he saw were numbingly familiar, but now most of them seemed like props on a stage: canisters of insecticide locked in a case against the wall, shelves lined with books dedicated to the fine art of insect extermination, and a supposedly amusing plastic mosquito that boogied to a shrill snippet of Sinatra crooning "I've Got You Under My Skin" when you walked within a foot of it.

"They've been lying to me," said Billy. "My whole life, they've been lying to me."

He glanced at Piker again.

"Even my *dog* has been lying to me."

Piker groaned and curled up into a ball.

Billy went back to staring at the TV, through the TV. There was a tiny sliver of popcorn kernel stuck between his teeth. He'd been unsuccessfully trying to dislodge it for the last hour and a half.

"Well, they won't get away with it, I can tell you that much. They're going to apologize. They're going to explain. They're going to make it up to me."

Piker groaned.

"And I'm going to take my good, sweet time forgiving them."

He paused, then continued: "If I *decide* to forgive them. As a twelve-year-old who has been lied to every single year of his entire twelve-year-long life . . ." Billy's sentences weren't holding together as well as they normally did. ". . . I reserve the right to *not* forgive. To withhold forgiveness. For *years.*"

The sliver of popcorn kernel was tantalizingly close to coming free. But it stayed put.

"Forever, if necessary."

BRRRUUUUUMMMmmmmm

The van. That's them!

Billy jumped up from the couch, ran through the kitchen

to the back door, and yanked it open. There in the driveway was the creaky old BUGZ-B-GON van. He got there just in time to see the headlights go out.

G'JUNK G'JUNK

Jim and Linda Clikk got out of the van. They were dressed in the same gray uniforms Twain and the others had worn. The only source of light in the backyard was an outdoor bulb jutting out from the aluminum siding of their two-story colonial. Its blinding white light sent long black shadows crawling off behind Jim and Linda and stretching out across the driveway. Crickets chirped in the bushes, and the smell of wet grass hung in the air.

Jim's face seemed to have creases in places it hadn't before. His eyes were pinched with uncertainty, and his high-and-mighty jaw was nearly touching his chest. Linda was fidgety and fragile-looking. She blinked excessively, and her cheeks were a splotchy, feverish red.

They began walking toward Billy, moving slowly and cautiously, as if they were creeping up on a fizzled firecracker that might still blow. Neither of them spoke until they were close enough to reach out and touch him.

"Son," Jim Clikk said, "I guess we have some explaining to do."

On an ordinary night, Billy would have laughed out loud at the ridiculousness of this remark. It was, after all, one of the most monstrous understatements of all time. But this was not an ordinary night. Billy scowled and remained silent.

"Please don't be angry, Billy," Linda said. Her face was twisted with guilt. "We were going to tell you just as soon as you turned sixteen." She paused and added: "Or fifteen. You're twelve now, so that's not such a long time, really, when you . . . when you think about it."

I can't believe this. As if that makes any difference!

"Liars," Billy said. "You guys are liars."

"Yes," Jim said. Always better than Billy's mother at

putting on a brave face, he nevertheless appeared thoroughly off balance, unsure of how to proceed. "We *are* liars, there's no getting around that. But we're *good* liars. I mean," he added before clearing his throat, "liars for good reasons. Look, why don't we just go inside, make a few nice mugs of cocoa, and—"

"No!" said Billy, with an intensity that had neighbor-waking potential. The crickets silenced themselves. Jim and Linda recoiled, raising their hands like criminals trying to prove they were unarmed.

Billy lowered his voice but sounded just as angry. "No cocoa. I don't want cocoa. I want . . ." It took him a second to put it into words.

I want things to go back to normal.

No. I don't want that. Normal wasn't so great. In fact, it sucked a lot of the time.

I want . . . to be in on everything.

He started over. "Look. I've got questions. Lots and lots of questions. I'm going to ask my questions and you're going to answer them, one at a time."

Billy's parents glanced at each other, turned back to him, and nodded solemnly. The crickets cautiously resumed their chirping.

"And no more lies. Ever."

"No more lies," his parents said, as if taking an oath. "Ever."

"Okay," said Billy. The sliver of popcorn came free at last, and he spat it onto the lawn.

CHAPTER 6

They wound up sitting around the kitchen table, a bowl of un-popped popcorn kernels serving as a sort of centerpiece. The smell of butter was mixed with whiffs of chicken curry, creating an aroma Billy might have found rather agreeable if he hadn't been sick to his stomach from everything he'd gone through in the last few hours. The refrigerator hummed noisily beneath it all, like a broken pipe organ playing one endless note.

"Now, let me get this straight," Billy said. His parents had been talking for over half an hour and hadn't even come close to answering all his questions. Of course, it didn't help that every answer tended to plant entirely new questions in his head. "You guys have just come back from the Philippines."

"That's right," Linda said. "We were there from early

yesterday morning until about eight o'clock last night." By this time she had tried to explain to Billy that keeping their work secret from him was not a mean-spirited trick. It was a way of protecting him, a way of ensuring that he would have a normal carefree childhood, free from the dangers his parents faced on a daily basis. (Billy was unimpressed.)

She'd told Billy that she and his father were performing an important service to the world, and that Billy's patience with their being away all the time was, in a very real sense, an essential part of that service. (Billy was unmoved.)

And she'd apologized. More than a dozen times and in a dozen different ways she'd apologized to Billy. For the lies, for the deceptions, for all the times he'd been left at home alone, and for the series of events that had led to his having five strange people crash through his bedroom window. But Billy was withholding forgiveness just as he'd pledged to, and so his mother finally stopped apologizing and switched to simply supplying him with as much information as possible.

Billy, for his part, had temporarily set aside some of his anger—about half of it, roughly—to concentrate on putting together the bizarre, secretive jigsaw puzzle of his parents' actual day-to-day lives.

"You were in the Philippines from early yesterday morning," he said, sounding like an attorney taking notes for an upcoming trial, "until about eight o'clock last night." He drew a breath before launching into the next sentence. This was the big one: the one that explained everything and yet was so utterly unbelievable as to be difficult to say while keeping a straight face. "You were sent to the Philippines . . ."

He inhaled and exhaled long and slow before continuing.

". . . as members of a secret society that battles things called creatches . . ."

Another deep breath.

". . . which are, basically . . ."

Another deep breath.

". . . *monsters.*"

"Yes," Linda said. "That's right." She was staring into Billy's eyes, speaking slowly, as if trying to help him accept all this. "Our job is to stop them from interfering with humans."

"So you're saying that monsters . . . are real. That the world is filled with monsters."

"Filled?" said Jim Clikk. He had apologized to Billy a grand total of twice, then abandoned that tactic in favor of answering questions, smiling a lot, and making heroic attempts to buck up everyone's spirits. To anyone else it would have seemed that Jim Clikk didn't like apologizing, or simply didn't care. Billy knew better, though. He knew his father was good at reading people, and that he'd taken one look at his son and understood that Billy was more interested in information than apologies.

"No," Jim continued. "I wouldn't say that the world is *filled* with monsters. There are a lot of them, though. Plenty enough to keep us busy." He chuckled in a way that suggested it was no joke. "They live underground and in the oceans. On mountaintops, in forests, and in the sky."

"Monsters. Real monsters." Billy kept saying the word. He was trying to get used to it. He sensed that until he could come to grips with this fact—this thoroughly ridiculous-sounding fact—the jigsaw puzzle could never be put together.

"Oh yes," Jim said. "They're real, all right. Very real. Of course, they don't *think* of themselves as monsters. At least not in a very . . . monstery way."

Billy tried to imagine what these real monsters looked like. He saw flashes of things—claws, teeth, eyes, tails—but found it hard to put it all together into one complete beast.

"And, uh, how long has this secret society been around?"

"Centuries," Linda said. "It's existed in different forms—

and under a variety of names—since prehistoric times. You know the story of Saint George and the dragon?"

Billy didn't, really. "I've heard of it."

"Old George was an Affy, just like your father and me."

"Affy?"

"A member of AFMEC," Jim said, "the Allied Forces for the Management of Extraterritorial Creatches. Your mother and I have been senior AFMEC agents since 1988," he added, raising his jaw proudly.

"I know. I read that on your business card." Billy narrowed his eyes. "Your *real* business card." Billy's father winced and tried to smile. Only half of his mouth cooperated in the effort.

Billy cleared his throat and asked a question he was more than a little scared to have answered. "Were you two *ever* real exterminators? Or has BUGZ-B-GON always been a big show, just a, a . . . a way of hiding your secret identity?" Billy found it hard to use the phrase *secret identity* in a conversation with his parents. Somehow it sounded even weirder than using the phrase *real monsters* in a conversation with his parents.

Jim and Linda exchanged troubled glances. Linda leaned back in her chair, signaling that the question had fallen into Jim's territory.

"Um," Jim began, and for a moment it sounded as if Billy

was in for a long, complicated answer. Then his father let all the air out of his lungs and simply said: "Big show." He paused and added, "Secret identity," as if that might somehow soften the blow.

Billy scooted his chair back away from the table, producing a *dut-dut-dut*ting sound. He'd been preparing himself for this possibility. Still, it made him lose his breath for a second.

The funny thing was it didn't make him angry. Far from it. Deep down he had to admit he was impressed.

They didn't just fool me, they fooled the whole town: the neighbors, the police, everyone. These AFMEC people are cool. Way cool.

He definitely wanted to know more. Heck, he wanted to know everything.

"What about the answering machine here in the house? Sometimes people call and leave messages. You know, termite problems and stuff. What happens to those people? Do they ever get called back?"

"Right," said Jim. He shot a glance at Linda, and Billy immediately sensed that replying to his question, if done thoroughly, could take hours. "Okay. See, there's a whole big division of AFMEC called the NCPD: the Normal Childhood

Preservation Department. They make it possible for the children of Affys to lead normal lives up until the age of fifteen or sixteen. There's a group of men and women there who send mail, make phone calls, even drive by the house to drop off things 'from work,' you name it. It's all part of ensuring that the son or daughter believes his parents do the ordinary boring jobs they claim to do. It's hard work, but important."

"You mean that message last week about the fire ants at the Piffling Rotary Club . . ."

"That was Mamadou Diouf, one of the guys at the NCPD," said Jim. "He does a pretty good American accent, doesn't he? You'd never know he was born and raised in Senegal."

What an operation! These Affys had really worked out all the angles.

"So why does AFMEC have to be a big secret? Why can't you just . . . get everything out in the open?"

"Well," said Linda, "there's world tourism, for starters."

"*Tourism?* You've *got* to be kidding me."

"Think about it, Billy," she said. "If ordinary people knew about the creatches . . . all the nasty, saber-toothed, tentacled, bloodsucking beasts out there just beyond their range of vision . . . there'd be so much panic in the world no one would go anywhere. The human race would be crippled by its own fears." She paused, then added in a half-whisper: "They don't *all* suck blood. Very few of them do, actually."

"This is total insanity," Billy said. "If there are monsters out there, people need to know about it. Otherwise they'll get themselves into . . . you know . . . life-or-death situations without even realizing it."

"Not since the World Creach Accord of 1815," said Jim.

"You mean *1816,* dear," said Linda.

"Right," said Jim, waving the fact away like a pesky mosquito. "See, that was when AFMEC leaders and creach leaders got together and divided the world into human territories and creach territories. Since then, humans and creaches have coexisted in peace and harmony to a remarkable degree. AFMEC steps in only when a few bad apples cross the boundaries and start causing trouble."

Creach leaders. At a meeting.

Billy thought this over. "So these creaches must be pretty sophisticated. They've got their own government, and leaders, and they can attend meetings and stuff. So are they just as smart as human beings?"

"Some of them are *nearly* as smart as humans," Linda said. "But most possess no more intelligence than, say, your average insect. And as for a government, well, they *are* loosely organized, yes. The smarter ones use a variety of techniques to police the rest of them, ensuring that they stay out of human-controlled territories. Still, there are the inevitable transgressions. Like yesterday in the Philippines."

"Mutating slimewarblers," said Jim. "Ugly things. And they don't smell so hot either."

"Mutating slimewarblers. Is that what all that purple gunk was in the video? Mutating slime?"

"Yeah, and *that* was the part of town that was relatively unscathed," Jim said. "You should have seen the sports arena where they made their last stand. It was like a mountain of purple pudding."

Linda shuddered.

"Okay," said Billy, "but I still don't see how you can keep creatches secret after something like this. Didn't some of the locals *see* the slimewarblers?"

"Yes," said Linda. "It happens quite often. But AFMEC coordinates with local hospitals to have such people treated by Affy doctors rather than ordinary doctors. They get injected with a chemical called Somniron—a sort of memory inhibitor—that blurs their perceptions, makes them think it was all just a terribly vivid dream."

"You're able to round up *everyone*? Don't people get away sometimes?"

"On occasion, yes," said Linda. "Then you end up with

people going to the press. Nine times out of ten the newspeople think they're stark raving mad. The rest of the time you end up with a small story about how someone claims they saw an alien invader. Or Bigfoot."

"So there really *is* a Bigfoot," said Billy.

"Oh, there are loads of them," said Linda. "Well, technically they're called black-furred woodwalkers, but you can't expect your average moose hunter to know that."

Billy paused to take in this new information. He was trying to stay angry at his parents—he had good reason to, after all—but AFMEC was absolutely the coolest thing he'd ever heard of in his life. The more he found out about it, the more he wanted to know.

"So who's in charge of all you Affys?" he asked. "The president?"

"Of the United States?" Linda chuckled, as if the very idea were preposterous. "AFMEC is a global organization, darling. It doesn't belong to any one country or answer to any one government. It was formed from a variety of creach-battling groups that arose spontaneously all over the world in centuries past—China, Europe, South America. Today it's presided over by a prime magistrate: an elected official who could just as easily be from Wallonia as Washington, D.C."

Jim Clikk gave his wife a curious look. "Where's Wallonia?"

"Southern Belgium."

"Guys," said Billy, "let's try to stay on topic here, all right?"

Jim Clikk glanced at the clock on the wall and gently raised a finger. "Billy, these are good questions. *Great* questions. And we're going to keep answering them until you have all the info you need. And then some. But right now"—he leaned forward, striking a delicate balance between being buddy-buddy and reasserting his authority as Dad—"I'm under direct orders to touch base with HQ as soon as possible. So just where exactly did you find my viddy-fo—my, uh, business card case?"

"It's all right, Dad. I know what a viddy-fone is."

"You do?"

"Well, I have the general idea. It's like a miniature video-phone for all of you Affys."

"That's right."

"It was behind your dresser. I left it next to the phone."

"The dresser," Jim said, snapping his fingers and rising from his chair. "I *knew* it. All right, then. I'd better go get the little doodly-hickey and find out what they want us to do with you."

"*Do* with me?"

Jim stopped and rested a hand on Billy's shoulders. "Those Affys who crashed through your bedroom window weren't kidding, Billy. You broke some rules. You *did* do an impersonation of me on the phone, didn't you? A darned good one, I'm told."

Billy felt his face grow warm.

"And good impersonation or not," Jim continued, "that's a violation of code 574, section six, paragraph two."

I broke rules. They're going to do something to me.

"This is ridiculous!" Now that his question-and-answer session was being officially shut down, Billy's anger was back with a vengeance. "I didn't know anything about codes and rules when I made that phone call. Thanks to *you* two, I was completely in the dark!"

"You're right," said his mother. "This is our fault, and we're sorry for it. Deeply, truly sorry. You haven't deliberately done anything wrong. But . . ." She paused, struggling to find the right words. ". . . this is bigger than just the three of us, Billy. Rules are rules. Rules were broken. And there is a price to be paid for that."

Billy swallowed hard.

They're going to lock me up. Or torture me. Maybe they'll feed me to a creatch. . . .

"I'm sure they'll be lenient with you, darling," Linda said, as if reading his mind. "You're only twelve years old, for heaven's sake. They won't . . . hurt you or anything."

"They?"

"AFMEC high command," said Jim. "They're the ones who sent Twain and his squadron here to check you out. What'd you think of Twain, anyway? He's pretty hardcore, isn't he?"

"I . . . wasn't too crazy about the guy."

"Yeah, well, social skills aren't his strong suit. He's a good Affy, though. And a hard worker. Makes Linda and me look like slackers," Jim added as he trotted up the stairs.

"Try not to think too much about the punishment, Billy," said Linda. "Nothing bad is going to happen to you."

Billy swallowed again.

His mother rose from the table and carried the bowl of popcorn kernels to the sink. She sighed and tried to sound casual. "Remember that time you broke Daddy's ten-speed the day after he bought it? How did we punish you?"

"You didn't," Billy said. "You just told me to be more careful next time."

"Oh." She paused, with a confused look on her face, and then dumped the kernels in the trash can. She plunked the bowl down on the counter, crossed the kitchen to where Billy was sitting, and placed her hand on his shoulder.

"Listen, honey," she said. "I know it's hard for you after . . . all this . . . to trust your father and me. I don't blame you if you can't believe anything I'm saying to you right now. But this is the truth: I won't let them hurt you. I won't let them lock you up. I won't let them separate you from your father and me."

Billy looked deeply into his mother's eyes. She was telling the truth. There was no doubt about that.

"We thought we were doing something good for you by keeping AFMEC secret all these years. We were wrong about that. Dead wrong. I wish we could go back and undo that decision, I really do. But things are going to be different, Billy. From now on, we're sticking together, all three of us. You're in now."

"In?"

"In," Linda repeated. "In the know. Starting tonight, you're going to know everything that's going on, as it's going on. You'll know where we are, what we're doing, and how to get in touch with us if you need to. You'll never be in the dark again."

As she said these last words, her voice trembled a little. She leaned forward and gave Billy a hug: a big, strong, warm one that lasted for a full minute. For once, Billy didn't feel embarrassed or try to pull away.

CHAPTER 7

Jim came bounding down the stairs. "All right, you two. High command wants us at HQ right away. We've really got to skedaddle."

Billy's parents led him out to the BUGZ-B-GON van. Once before—when their other car was in the shop—Billy had been forced to ride with them in the van. He'd sworn it would be the last time. It was crammed from front to back with cardboard boxes, insecticide canisters, and tangled wheels of plastic tubing. There were no seats of any kind, just a cold rusty floor. He was barely able to squeeze in, and even then it meant getting whacked in the head over and over again by a loose piece of plywood.

Jim pulled the van door back, revealing that very same wall

of junk, all the objects in the same positions they had occupied before.

"Watch this," he said.

He flicked a switch and . . .

FSSSSSHHHHHHHhhhhhhhhhhhh

. . . the boxes and canisters began to shrink, collapse, and rise into the ceiling. It was as if all of it were made from inflatable plastic and were now having the air sucked out of it. Within a few seconds the rear of the van was completely clear of clutter, leaving only two swivel chairs (bolted to the floor), a wall of sleek metal drawers and lockers, and a small desk area that looked like a hyper-high-tech home office. There were four or five different computer screens and dozens of flashing lights.

"Whoa" was all Billy could say. He'd always been embarrassed by his parents' clunky old van. Now he was suddenly envying them: what a ride!

"Not bad, huh?" Jim said with a wink.

As Billy climbed in and strapped himself into one of the chairs, his father made a whistling sound and Piker came trotting out to join them. She still had a very anxious look on her face.

"Don't worry, Orzy," Jim said, scratching her behind the ears. "We know you did your best. I'll put in a good word for you with high command."

This seemed to cheer up Piker—or Orzamo, which Billy had now concluded was her real name—and she leaped into the van with more energy than she'd exhibited in several hours.

Wait a minute: if she understood English so well, how come she never seemed to understand the words sit *and* roll over?

Laziness, he concluded. *Then again, if I were a dog that understood English, I probably wouldn't be so crazy about sitting and rolling over either.*

Once everyone was inside, Jim revved the engine and sent them tearing off down Dullard Road.

"Mom, what does all this stuff do?" Billy asked as he stared at the array of buttons and dials on the desk.

"Some of it's for locating creatches," Linda said. "Some of it recommends strategies for dealing with specific creatch species. Some of it operates . . . well, weaponry." She smiled and added: "Don't touch anything, okay?"

Billy nodded quickly and folded his hands in his lap.

Now they were rumbling down a dirt road in the middle of Dullard Woods. It was a road hardly anyone ever drove on, since it was riddled with potholes and trailed off into a marshy dead end.

"How long will it take to get to AFMEC headquarters?" asked Billy. "A couple of days?"

"Days? I sure *hope* not." Jim chuckled. "Provided the wind

currents are in our favor, we should be there in two and a half hours."

Billy was about to ask what in the world wind currents had to do with a van on a dirt road when he noticed that the ride had become dramatically smoother. Not because the road was becoming less bumpy—far from it—but because the wheels of the van were no longer touching the road.

"We're . . ." Billy was too amazed to even finish the sentence.

"Airborne?" his mother said. "Yes, that's right. It's called transgravitational propulsion. Perfected by AFMEC back in the sixties. It's far superior to conventional air travel—a lot less noisy, for one thing." Indeed, they were coasting through the air in absolute silence.

Billy stared wide-eyed out the small square windows in the back of the van. He saw the treetops of Dullard Woods rolling underneath them like a green leafy sea. In the distance were the dimly lit windows of Piffling's tiny downtown, and beyond them, the waters of Lake Flawatamee.

"A flying van," said Billy to whoever could hear him. "I'm sitting inside a flying van."

"That you are, Billy boy," said his father, popping a CD into the dashboard. "I've been wanting to take you up in this thing for years. So far as I'm concerned, there's really no other way to travel."

"Oh, man. You have *got* to teach me how to fly this thing."

"Whoa, whoa, whoa," said Jim. "Take it easy, little man. You don't even have a driver's license yet."

"Come on, Dad. I'll be careful."

"I'll make you a deal. Be a good kid, get decent grades in school, and I'll let you take her for a little spin on your next birthday."

Fair enough, thought Billy. *But flying the van is just the beginning. I want to get in on all this creatch-battling stuff. I mean, talk about extreme sports: messing with monsters is about as extreme as you can get. I bet it's the ultimate rush.*

Billy turned his attention to a series of strange weapons kept in a glass case attached to one of the walls. There were the same pear-shaped pistols he'd seen Twain and his crew use, but there were other things that looked even weirder. One was a disk covered with spikes and made of steel polished to a mirrorlike finish: from the looks of it, a sort of lethal Frisbee. Another was long, curved, and engraved with intricate spidery carvings, like a bazooka from another planet. Still others didn't look like weapons at all: they were soft and rubbery, and dangling from hooks.

I want to learn how to use all this stuff. It's gotta be so sweet to get out there with the creatches, blasting them with these things. I wonder if you get to keep body parts as souvenirs. Probably not. Still, just knowing you took one of them down . . . it must be the most awesome feeling on earth.

The van was suddenly filled with the psychedelic guitar music of Abstruse Muse, an obscure seventies rock band his father was crazy about for some reason. Normally Billy would immediately beg him to shut it off, but for the moment he was too fascinated with the view out the back window. They were now high above the Indiana countryside and the tiny yellow lights of farmhouse windows and backroad streetlamps slowly crawled past beneath them.

Linda handed him a stick of gum wrapped in silver foil. "For the altitude," she said.

He unwrapped the gum and popped it in his mouth. "These AFMEC people must be rolling in dough," he said. "They make their own antigravity vans. Their own viddy-fones. Even their own chewing gum!"

"Almost every country on Earth has a contract with AFMEC," Linda said, "and governments don't quibble about what it costs, as long as their lands are kept creach free. So AFMEC's got money, yes. But they don't make their own chewing gum."

"They don't?"

"No. This is Juicy Fruit."

"Oh."

They began to pick up speed. The clouds flew past, and by the time they'd reached "Parade of the Paisley Pantaloons"—the eighth track on the CD—Linda said they were already over the Pacific Ocean.

"So where exactly *is* AFMEC headquarters?" Billy asked.

"For a long time it was in the side of a mountain in Tibet," Jim replied. "Then some hikers stumbled across it and they had to relocate. From around '91 until '93 they had temporary digs in Antarctica."

"Hoo, was it cold," said Linda.

"Yeah, Affys weren't too crazy about that. Now they've found the perfect hideaway: the Pacific Ocean."

"The *ocean*? What, it's underwater?"

"Yes, but very near the surface. You'll see. Better get some sleep, Billy. This is going to be a long day." Billy's father switched off the music and punched a button on the dashboard. A small bunk rose from the floor in the back of the van.

Billy didn't want to sleep. He had never wanted so badly to stay awake. But it was the middle of the night, and he was exhausted, there was no getting around that.

I'll close my eyes for a couple of minutes, he thought. *Just to get my energy back.*

He was asleep in five minutes.

When he opened his eyes, blinding yellow sunlight was pouring into the van. He was startled, then relieved as he realized where he was.

"Rise and shine, honey," Linda said. "We're almost there."

Billy rubbed his face and shielded his eyes from the glare. The van began to bank and turn away from the sun, making it easier to see the dazzling view beyond the windshield: bright green ocean and blue morning sky. Billy searched for signs of an entrance to AFMEC headquarters but saw nothing except water and white-capped waves.

His heart was beating faster. Discovering the flying van had been a mind bender, all right, but now he was heading into something so amazing he was having trouble picturing it: an inhabitable headquarters located entirely underwater. Billy wondered if it was some kind of submarine or if it looked more like a giant aquarium.

"Now, remember, son," Jim said, "the fact that they've asked us to bring you to headquarters is a pretty big deal. You're in trouble, yes. But you're also being checked out."

"Checked out?"

"AFMEC membership, whenever possible, is handed down from generation to generation. It's part tradition, part biological necessity. We Affys need to possess certain genes that allow us to withstand the rigors of creach battling. Ever notice how your scrapes and scratches heal quicker than other kids'?"

"Sure," said Billy. When he and Nathan went out skateboarding all over Piffling and came back with the bloodied shins to prove it, Billy's cuts always healed a day or two ahead of Nathan's. "I always figured it was just 'cause other guys pick at their scabs more than I do."

"Don't kid yourself, son. You pick at your scabs plenty. I've seen you."

Billy rolled his eyes.

"No sirree. It's your Affy blood. It's come down to you from generations of Affys on both sides of your family. I got it from my parents just the way you got it from your mother and me."

"Wait a minute. You mean Grandpa was an Affy?"

"Oh, sure. And his father before him."

Billy thought this over. His grandfather had died about five years earlier. His grandmother, though, was still alive and well.

"What about Gramma?"

His mother turned to face him. "She was one of the best. She could have been the Affy prime magistrate if not for the prejudices of the day."

"Gramma?" It was really hard to imagine. Billy's grandmother was a frail old woman with a hunched back and squinty hazel eyes who got around using two canes. She looked as if she'd lose a fight with a garden hose, let alone a monster.

"You'll see," said Linda. "Next time we go visit, she'll tell you all about the creatches she dealt with back in the thirties. Once she gets started, there'll be no stopping her."

Checked out. Handed down from generation to generation. Did Dad mean they might want to turn *Billy* into an Affy? Well, of course he did. What *else* could he mean?

Yes! But how soon will they let me join? Am I still gonna have to wait until I'm fifteen? Man, I hope not. I want to start right now. Okay, so I did a little impersonation of Dad on the phone. They're not gonna hold that against me, are they?

Suddenly Billy felt as if there was nothing on earth he'd rather be than an Affy. As if it was what he'd wanted to do all his life.

I want to know all the lingo. I want my own viddy-fone. I want to learn how to fly the van and use all these freaky weapons. And I definitely *want to see some action with a creatch. Maybe just a small one to get started. Still, nothing too cute. Gimme one about the size of a cow, but with really sharp teeth.*

"All right," Jim said, "this is it." He steered the van down toward a tiny rock sticking up from the waves. You couldn't really call it an island. It was no larger than a baseball diamond. The waves smacked up against it on all sides, sending towers of spray into the air.

Jim brought the van in for a gentle landing and killed the engine. For a moment they just sat there listening to the waves pounding the rock. The saltwater smell reminded Billy of trips to the beach.

K'CHUNK

There was a noise from the underside of the van, as if something hard and metallic had reached up and grabbed hold of it by the axles.

A crackle of static from the dashboard, then:

"How do you find my pickled radishes?" said the voice of a tin can woman, serious but slightly bored.

Jim leaned back in his seat, allowing Linda to answer the question.

"They're fine with rice, but foul with barley." She turned to Billy. "That's the password. For today, anyway. They'll have a new one at the stroke of midnight."

"How your mother remembers them," said Jim with an admiring sigh, "is beyond me."

CHZZZZZzzzzz

A buzz filled Billy's ears and the whole van lurched backward a foot or two.

"Hold on, Billy," Linda said. "They're taking us down."

CHAPTER 8

It all happened so quickly that Billy would have missed it if he'd blinked at the wrong time. The van tilted backward, dropped through a trapdoor in the surface of the rock, and shot down into a vast space below. It was a controlled fall: they were gliding along a track like a car on a roller coaster.

Billy peered through the windshield and struggled to make sense of what he was seeing. A thick wall of glass rose on all sides, enclosing a vast manmade world beneath the waves. The sun's rays poured in from above, blue-green and wavering like light at the bottom of a swimming pool.

Un. Be. Lievable. Look at the size *of this place!*

The rock they had been resting on just seconds before was fake: a secret entrance at the top of an enormous underwater city. Billy guessed the whole complex was at least three miles from one side to the other, and nearly a mile from top to bottom.

The van rolled noiselessly along the track, slowly circling the entire dome as it descended into a cluster of buildings that would have been the envy of any city on earth. There were glistening white office towers dozens of stories tall, along with older buildings that looked as if they'd been disassembled and moved in from various regions of the world. There were people walking through green parks lined with leafy trees and spacious plazas with fountains spouting water high into the air. There were roadways that carried shiny gray vehicles throughout the city and shimmering glass tubes that allowed foot traffic to pass from one high-rise to another. There were even narrow strips of farmland squeezed in between buildings.

This is the coolest place in the world, and practically no one even knows it's here! Now I gotta become an Affy, so I can hang out here all the time. I wonder if they'd let me bring my skateboard. . . .

"AFMECopolis," said Jim. "The air gets a little stuffy down here—something to do with the oxygen filtration system—but you can't beat the view. Especially when the whales go by."

The van coasted down to a wide concrete platform that was like a huge helicopter pad. It was about five hundred feet across, with several ramps attached to it that led to nearby parking garages. There were two vehicles already on the platform. One was a shiny red Porsche; the other was an old yellow school bus covered with dents and rust spots. "The school bus is actually faster than the Porsche," said Jim. "Sports cars don't handle the air turbulence so well."

They came to an abrupt stop and all the doors on the van opened automatically. Orzamo jumped out and stood next to the van. Billy followed her and immediately began turning his head in every direction. Several vehicles swooshed past on a ramp below. A building off to one side towered above them, covering half the platform in shadow. The sunlight—twice muted, by the water and the superthick glass above—tinted his skin a pale blue.

Billy inhaled deeply. His father was right. The air was slightly stuffy. Humid.

He peered up at the glass dome above and shuddered.

Man, I hope they've never had any problems with it cracking.

"Back already, Mr. Clikk? You were just here yesterday." A whiskered old man in overalls trotted out from a nearby doorway. He had a green-and-orange parrot on his shoulder. Or a parrot-like animal, anyway. Billy noticed with delight that it had scales on its belly, like a fish, and five or six spikes jutting out of its head.

"So what is it this time," the old man asked, "special business, or another creatch op?" He was examining the front of the van and hadn't noticed Billy yet.

"I guess you'd have to call it special business." Jim wrapped an arm around Billy's shoulder and scooted him forward. "Gordy, I'd like you to meet my son."

The old man flinched as if a pistol had been pulled on him. The parrot creature flapped its wings and let out the piercing yowl of a startled house cat. Several more spikes popped out of its head, only to begin receding seconds later, and its wings turned from green to red.

"Holy smokes," the old man said, stroking the parrot creature's head to calm it down. "This *is* special business. What's goin' on here, Mr. Clikk?"

"Long story, Gordy. We'll fill you in later."

They crossed to an escalator at the edge of the platform, Orzamo trotting along behind them. The old man called out to Jim as the escalator carried them up and away: "How's she flyin', Mr. Clikk?" He was back to examining the van.

"Straight as an arrow, Gordy," Jim called back, raising an enthusiastic thumb into the air.

"Actually," he whispered to Billy a moment later, "she's still a little wobbly from a mission we had in Alaska a few weeks back. I'll tell you all about it someday. Hair-raising stuff."

"Stuff involving two hundred and fifty pounds of salmon heads?"

Now it was Jim who flinched. "How did you . . . find out about that?"

Billy smiled. "Come on, Dad. You left the receipt in the trash can."

Jim looked irritated and pleased at the same time.

When they reached the top of the escalator, they crossed a marble-floored lobby toward a bank of elevators. To get there they had to weave through dozens of Affys charging from one place to another: people of all races, shapes, and sizes, but all dressed in the same gray AFMEC uniform. Orzamo led the way, bounding through the various obstacles with astonishing speed and grace.

Jim and Linda followed, and Billy brought up the rear, checking out the walls above as he went along. They were painted with murals depicting what appeared to be Affy exploits through the ages: ancient Chinese Affys battling a huge red blob near the Great Wall, Inuit Affys firing harpoons at a slick-skinned amphibious creature in the thick of a snowstorm, Mexican Affys chasing a herd of fire-breathing black lizards across a cactus-covered plain.

Billy was so busy gazing up at the murals, he nearly crashed into something as it glided by on a pushcart: a large aquarium filled with multiarmed translucent creatures bobbing slowly up and down in a yellowish liquid. They were about two feet tall from top to bottom, with bodies like jellyfish and pink pulsing organs visible right through the skin. They had at least half a dozen eyes apiece, some of which slowly opened and closed as the aquarium rolled past.

Suddenly one of the creatures slid a slimy arm out of the aquarium and wrapped it around Billy's neck. It was frigid and wet against his skin, like a dead salamander. There was a nauseating chemical smell too, like a freshly dissected frog.

Billy reached up and tried to throw the thing off him, but it already had a pretty good grip.

"Mom! Dad!"

Billy's parents turned just as the arm stretched to its limit and let go, slithering back to the aquarium, which disappeared down a nearby corridor.

"Whoops," said Linda with a chuckle. "Jellied bagflabbits. They do that sometimes. No harm done, eh?" she added as she inspected Billy's neck and wiped a bit of the slime from his shirt.

"That was pretty disgusting," said Billy. "But kinda cool, too. I just made contact with my first creach."

"That you did, my boy," said Jim. "If only all the other creaches were as harmless as those bagflabbits. They were pretty heavily sedated," he added with a wink.

When Billy and his parents joined Orzamo on the other side of the lobby, Linda punched an impossibly long series of numbers into a keypad on the wall. As she did, a fellow Affy passed and smiled. He looked Chinese.

"Linda, *nǐ hǎo!*" he said.

"*Chén xiānshēng,*" Linda said, still punching numbers into the pad, "*hǎo jiǔ bù jiàn!*" She spoke with a perfect Chinese accent. Well, perfect to Billy's ears, anyway.

Jim smiled proudly and squatted down to pat Orzamo on the head. "We'll be right back down, girl," Jim said. The dog sighed and found a place to sit at the edge of the lobby.

While they waited for the elevator doors to open, Billy

glanced up and noticed that the entire wall above them was covered with bronze plaques—hundreds of them—some shiny and new, others tarnished with age. He read three of the plaques nearest him:

Abubakari Nsubuga, Senior AFMEC Agent

*Agent Nsubuga was skinned alive while
rescuing stranded mountaineers from a
humpbacked akkle yak. Defective weaponry
forced him to fight the beast with his bare hands.
Seventeen lives were saved on that day; tragically,
Nsubuga's was not among them.*

June 14, 1902

Harriet M. Flannigan, Junior AFMEC Agent

*Agent Flannigan was flattened while
rescuing Mauritanian nomads from a five-ton rolling narmf.
She ensured the survival of dozens of men, women,
and children by luring the beast to the edge of a nearby precipice,
where she sent it plunging to its death,
but only after having made the ultimate sacrifice.
She died—as she lived—in the path of danger.*

October 11, 1988

Skinned alive? thought Billy. *Debrained? Man, these Affys are into some seriously dangerous stuff here. Even the agents-in-training buy it sometimes.*

Billy looked at his parents, and suddenly they seemed very different to him. They hadn't changed, of course. They were still the same people he'd always thought of as his dorky mom and dad. Now, though, they weren't dorks at all. They were like action heroes from a movie.

PING

Doors slid open and they stepped into one of the elevators. There were no buttons of any kind. Instead, there was a video monitor in the wall before them, a frumpy woman peering from it. She looked as if she needed coffee.

"Morning, Linda, Jim," she said. "This must be our little . . . prank caller."

Billy swallowed, wondering if he should say something.

"Good morning, Louise," Linda said. "Is Mr. Vriffnee ready to see us?"

"As ready as he'll ever be."

The screen went blank. The elevator began to rise.

"Now, listen, Billy," Linda said, "just leave the talking to us. Mr. Vriffnee is a good man . . ."

"A great man," added Jim.

". . . but he's not a very . . . patient man."

"Va-*riff*-nee?" Billy had never heard a name like it before.

"That's right." His mother smiled a nervous smile. "He's the boss. The prime magistrate of AFMEC. He's going to decide how you'll be . . ."

Her lips puckered.

". . . dealt with."

"You mean punished," said Billy.

Jim Clikk put a hand on Billy's shoulder and spoke to him with great seriousness, something he didn't often do.

"Listen to me, Billy. Whatever they do to you, I'm going to insist they do it to your mother and me too. We're in this together. And we're going to get through it together."

PING

The elevator doors opened.

CHAPTER 9

They stood in an office, much smaller than Billy had expected after the grandness of the lobby below. There were shelves covered with books, tables half hidden by maps unfurled across them, and bulletin boards buried under pieces of paper. Indeed, everything in the room seemed to be buried under something else.

In the corner was a desk. Behind the desk was a man. *Mr. Vriffnee,* thought Billy, and found that he had trouble pronouncing the name even in his mind.

"Get in here." The old man was facing a dusty computer screen, squinting through spectacles at tiny green letters scrolling across it.

Jim led the way, marching across the creaky wooden floor

to one of three chairs in front of the desk. He stood near it but didn't sit down. Billy and his mother did the same.

"Sit down."

They sat down.

A speaker nearby periodically erupted into snatches of conversation, like radio dispatches on a police officer's walkie-talkie: ". . . mountain creatches?" a staticky voice asked. "That's right," an equally staticky voice answered. "Lady says they've been in her barn for the last two weeks. . . . Over. . . ."

Mr. Vriffnee finally turned to face them and rocked back in his chair, which made a prolonged squeak. His thick spectacles magnified his eyes and the mass of wrinkles surrounding them. He had slightly disheveled white hair and a bushy white mustache to match.

He cleared his throat. "James. Linda."

Billy's parents leaned forward.

Mr. Vriffnee paused before continuing. His eyes swept back and forth as he regarded Billy's parents. Billy was both disappointed and relieved that the old man's eyes never met his.

"I've seen some serious breaches of security in my time. But I've never seen anything this . . . outrageous." He had a hint of an accent: German or Russian, maybe. Billy squirmed in his chair.

Jim raised an index finger. "I take full responsibility, Mr.

Vriffnee." He inhaled deeply, preparing for a long and carefully worded explanation. He never got the chance.

"You better *believe* you're taking full responsibility. Let's just take a look at this. *Together.*" Mr. Vriffnee hammered a button on his desk and one of the bulletin boards flipped up to reveal a silvery video screen. It flickered, then projected a scene that Billy found oddly familiar: Signs in foreign languages. Confetti. His parents in a convertible.

It was the same broadcast he'd seen on TV the previous evening.

"Do you have any idea . . . ," Mr. Vriffnee began, ". . . any *concept* of how many people saw this?" His eyebrows were drawn so close together they were getting tangled. Billy caught his mother giving his father an *I told you so* look.

"Well?" Mr. Vriffnee's face was red. He was shaking with anger.

"It was a small, lightly populated island," said Jim. "We were given assurances by the local authorities that the parade wouldn't even be *filmed*, much less broadcast on televi—"

"Assurances!" Mr. Vriffnee jumped up from his desk. *"Assurances!"* He began to storm around the room, sending pieces of paper whirling to the floor wherever he went. "A lot of good those assurances will do you when creatches start recognizing you wherever you go!"

Billy breathed a quiet sigh of relief and settled back to watch his parents get in trouble instead of him.

"Parades! Confetti!" Mr. Vriffnee pounded a table. A book fell off a shelf. "For the love of . . . You might as well paint a bull's-eye on your forehead and start inviting creatches over for dinner!"

Billy's parents were sitting there like kids sent to the principal's office. His father was biting his lip. His mother was examining her hands as if she'd never seen them before.

"You *know* how many creatch supremacists want you dead," said Vriffnee. "You're at the top of their list. Both of you!"

Creatches want Mom and Dad dead? thought Billy.

Vriffnee opened his mouth to continue but then stopped himself, as if he wanted his words to sink in a little more.

There was a long, uncomfortable silence. Billy became aware of a grandfather clock *tuk-tuk-tuk*king on the other side of the room. Next to it was a little bronze sculpture: a man dressed in a Roman toga thrusting a spear into a beast that was half ox, half scorpion.

The speaker crackled: "Hank, gimme an update on those sea creatches, will ya?" "Yeah, uh, we're definitely gonna need some reinforcements, Pete. They've sunk a couple of fishing boats out here, it's a real mess. . . ."

Mr. Vriffnee circled the room one last time and returned to

his desk. He planted his hands among the stacks of paper and gave Billy's parents an ugly stare. They sank lower in their chairs and turned their eyes to the floor.

"Listen. You're two of the best agents I've got. But look at yourselves." He rolled his eyes at the video screen. The footage of Billy's parents was being played over and over in an endless loop: they were smiling, waving, loving every minute of their moment in the spotlight. "You're like a couple of nitwits."

Billy had to stop himself from grinning: seeing his mom and dad get busted like this was actually kind of fun.

"And *you*."

Uh-oh. Billy bolted up in his chair. Mr. Vriffnee was staring directly at him.

"Unauthorized handling of AFMEC property. Impersonation of an Affy. Acquisition of restricted information." Mr. Vriffnee didn't look quite as angry as he had earlier. But even a not-quite-as-angry Mr. Vriffnee was pretty darned angry-looking.

"I could have you detained here indefinitely, young man. There's a special place in the AFMEC detention center for children like you. If you're so anxious to find out about what we do here, I could have you sharing a bunk with a delinquent demi-creatch. How would you like that?"

Billy swallowed and said nothing. He knew from experience that grown-ups didn't expect you to answer these sorts of questions, and became strangely angry when you did.

"But since this is a first-time offense, and since your actions were due mainly to the incompetence of an AFMEC member"—Mr. Vriffnee shifted his gaze to Jim, who sank even farther into his chair—"I'm going to be lenient."

Mr. Vriffnee shuffled some papers on his desk and took a quick glance at the computer screen he'd been reading earlier. Then he turned back to Billy and his parents, now seeming to regard them as nothing more than a bit of unfinished business.

"Take him back home," he said to Billy's parents, "and see to it that nothing like this ever—*ever*—happens again." Billy's parents nodded vigorously.

"As for these televised shenanigans of yours . . ." He was still talking to Billy's parents but was no longer looking at them. ". . . I'm placing you on involuntary leave for a month. Maybe a few weeks cooling your jets will teach you to take your AFMEC responsibilities a little more seriously."

Billy had never seen his parents look so heartbroken.

"That's it. I'll see you back here in a month."

Billy's parents rose to their feet, and Billy did the same. They all crossed back to the doors where the empty elevator waited for them. As they stepped inside, Jim placed a hand on Billy's shoulder. "Mr. Vriffnee went easy on you today, Billy. You should thank him."

Billy cleared his throat.

"Thank you, Mr. Very-funny."

Billy's parents gasped.

Mr. Vriffnee's gritted teeth and bulging black eyes were all Billy could see as the elevator doors slid shut.

CHAPTER 10

"I didn't *mean* to call him Very-funny. It just came *out* that way."

Billy was eating hot dogs with his parents in the AFMEC cafeteria. It was a brightly lit place that looked surprisingly like the food court at Piffling's local shopping mall, but with one important difference: a small-town food court generally doesn't have a display in the middle of it featuring an enormous stuffed creach. AFMEC's cafeteria did, and Billy couldn't stop staring at it. It was thirty feet tall, multi-eyed, and covered with horns.

"Of course you didn't, darling," Linda said. "No one in his right mind would intentionally call Mr. Vriffnee very funny." She was trying to sound cheerful. She and Jim looked depressed, though. There was no disguising it.

A silence fell over the table. Billy took another bite of hot dog. "Vita-dogs," his father had explained as they stood in line to get them. "Over seven hundred percent more vitamins and minerals than ordinary hot dogs." And boy, could you taste it. Every bite of vita-dog was like a mouthful of chalk. Still, the vita-dogs were downright tasty compared to the protein-enriched hypersprouts, dark green scraggly things that looked like spinach and tasted like fermented seaweed.

"Jimmy!" Billy spun around to see a tall, thin man striding across the cafeteria with his family behind him: a wife and daughter. The three of them were wearing matching AFMEC uniforms.

Billy's eyes immediately focused on the girl: she was the first person his own age he'd seen since leaving Piffling. Twelve years old, he figured, maybe thirteen. She was small with shoulder-length black hair, long eyelashes, and just a hint of freckles. He'd never seen anyone like her at Piffling Elementary, that was for sure. She was pretty. Like someone from a magazine ad. It was kind of disturbing.

"Jimmy, Linda! So good to see you two, it's been too long." The man had a thick South American accent. "And who do we have here?" He extended his arms and smiled at Billy like a long-lost uncle waiting for an overdue hug.

"Allow me to introduce you, Fernando," Jim Clikk said, rising from his chair. "This is our son, Billy."

Billy shook Fernando's big hairy hand as Linda and the woman exchanged kisses on the cheeks, then launched into what must have been a sidesplittingly funny conversation in fluent Spanish.

"Billy, this is Fernando García, his wife, Maria, and their daughter, Ana. They're from Guatemala."

Billy allowed his eyes to meet Ana's for a split second but immediately found he preferred looking somewhere else. Anywhere else.

"Ana's a little like you, Billy," Jim continued with a grin, "except that when *she* discovered what *you* discovered she was only seven years old. They tried to convince her to wait until she was older, but she insisted on starting early. Little Ana was just made a full-fledged Affy, what was it, a year ago?"

Ana rolled her eyes. She obviously wasn't too crazy about being called little Ana.

"Yes, yes," Fernando said, beaming with pride. "The youngest in the organization right now."

"But she'll not stay an Affy long," Maria said to Billy with mock seriousness, "if she doesn't improve the terrible grades she's been getting in school."

Ana ignored this remark and turned to Billy with an excited smile. "So you're an Affy too? We younger Affys have to stick together. Show the adults we're not as dumb as they think we are, you know?" She had an accent just like her parents, and spoke with that same *C'mon, let's be friends* tone of voice. Billy had dealt with her sort before. They were good-looking, they knew everything about everything, and they thought everyone they met should instantly adore them.

"I'm not an Affy," Billy said, trying to come up with a clever remark to follow this with but finding himself at an utter loss.

Linda put a reassuring hand on Billy's shoulder. "Give him time, Ana. He just found out about all this last night."

Oh, great, Mom, thought Billy. *Now she thinks I'm some kind of charity case.*

"It's going to take him a while to get used to things," Linda continued. "Then we can see if he wants to be an Affy or not."

"Oh, you will," said Ana. She moved closer to Billy, and for a moment he feared she might actually take a seat next to him. "Being an Affy is a lot of fun. It can be a little scary, depending on which creatch you're battling. And people *do* get bitten or even eaten alive sometimes, you know. . . ."

Billy wished she'd stop saying *you know*.

"Still, you're going to love it, I'm sure. Tell me if you need any help when your Affy entrance exams start. Some of those questions can be tricky, you know, especially the multiple choice and fill-in-the-blanks. I'd be happy to give you some tips."

Billy felt his face growing warm. *How can she talk to me like this? Like she's the big expert and I'm a nobody?*

"I wish we could stay, Jimmy," Fernando said, "but we're due in Vladivostok by the end of the day. Big creach op going on. Spotted scumspitters. It's getting pretty sticky over there."

Finally. They're leaving.

"Nice meeting you, Billy," said Ana. She touched him on the arm as she said it, and Billy suddenly found it impossible to say anything in return. He ended up producing a sound that was a cross between a cough and a gulp.

"Such a pretty young girl," Linda said after they were gone. "And smart as a whip. You should become friends with her, Billy. She could teach you a thing or two about creach battling, that's for sure."

I don't need her. I'm going to learn how to be an Affy on my own.

Jim Clikk waved his vita-dog in the air, trying to remember something. "Ana was the one who single-handedly captured the flesh-eating glabslug of Ouagadougou, wasn't she?"

"Yes," said Linda. "And at age nine. Very impressive."

"Can we talk about something else?" Billy said, and his parents smiled at each other for some reason.

Jim pointed his hot dog in Orzamo's direction. "Want some of this, Orzy?"

Orzamo grimaced, shook her head, and went back to examining a newspaper Linda had placed on the floor for her. Orzamo had always spent a lot of time nosing through newspapers and magazines back in Piffling (when she still went by the name of Piker). Billy had noticed it, along with many other distinctly undoglike habits of hers, and had been vaguely aware that there was something unusual about her. He had noticed these details but had never managed to string them all together or question what they all meant. Now, though, Billy saw plainly that the dog wasn't just looking at the newspaper. She was *reading* it.

"What's the deal with Orzamo?" Billy asked. "Is she super-intelligent or what?"

Billy's parents exchanged a glance. Jim made a face that suggested Linda had better handle this one.

"Orzamo is a demi-creatch," Linda explained. "An ordinary animal—in this case, a dog—crossbred with a creatch."

Billy's eyes widened.

"Don't worry, she's not dangerous. Not to us, anyway." Linda smiled at Orzamo, who smiled back and wagged her tail. "Demi-creatches are an important part of AFMEC's operation. We've managed to convert quite a lot of them to our cause."

"So she's smarter than an ordinary dog?"

Linda raised a finger: she had just taken a big bite of hot dog and needed time to chew and swallow. "Oh, yes. *Much* smarter. And that's just the beginning." She turned to Orzamo. "Go on, Orzy. Show Billy what you really look like."

Orzamo stood up on all fours and shook herself vigorously, as if she'd just stepped out of a tub full of water. When she stopped, she had changed in almost every respect: black fur had turned to yellow shiny skin; dog ears had turned to small, curved horns; and stubby paws had turned to three-toed chicken feet. She was now an exotic lizard, a miniature dinosaur with a tail the length of Billy's arm.

Billy's jaw dropped.

All traces of the dog he'd known as Piker were gone. Well, all but her long, wet tongue, which hung out of her mouth just as it always had, bobbing up and down as she panted in short doglike breaths.

"Creatch blood is dominant," Linda said. "Orzamo's forest creatch characteristics overpower her dog characteristics. If not for all the training she's undergone, she'd look like this all the time, even back home."

"Did you say *forest* creatch characteristics?"

"That's right. There are five different kinds of creatch. Forest creatches, which include tropical and jungle creatches. Ground creatches, which include desert, tundra, and subterranean creatches. Aquatic creatches, which can be found both in the oceans and in some large inland lakes. Mountain creatches, which limit themselves mainly to elevations of one thousand feet or higher. And air creatches, which share some habitat with mountain creatches but stay airborne for much of their lives.

"Orzamo's mother was an ordinary dog," Linda went on. "Her father was a forest creatch. Interbreeding between animals and creatches is very rare. The vast majority of creatches that encounter animals are more interested in eating them than mating with them. Luckily for us, Orzamo's father was one of the less aggressive creatches. He came across her mother—a terrier that had strayed into the forests of Saskatchewan—and evidently fell in love.

"Your father and I found all three of them by chance when we were on a creatch op outside Moose Jaw back before you were born. We brought them back to AFMECopolis, where Orzamo's parents stayed for many years. Her mother finally died ten years ago after a good long life. Orzamo's father died a couple years later."

Jim folded his hands behind his head and turned to Linda. "Isn't it great that we're finally able to tell him all this stuff?"

She smiled back. "Isn't it, though?"

Billy was down on all fours, examining Orzamo up close. "This is . . . incredible." He ran a hand across her back, marveling at the smooth reptile skin. Every so often he could hear a faint bleating sound, like the purring of an alien cat.

"Without Orzamo we'd never be able to leave you alone in Piffling like we do." Linda patted her mouth with a napkin. "That's her main job, actually: to protect you while we're gone. We hired Leo Krebs mainly just to reassure you that someone other than your dog was keeping an eye on you."

"You know, I've been thinking," Jim said. "This whole involuntary leave business is a blessing in disguise. This is our chance to make things right with Billy." Linda nodded enthusiastically.

Jim Clikk popped the last of his hot dog into his mouth and kept right on talking. "A month is not nearly enough to make up for what we've put you through all these years"—he pointed a finger at Billy—"but it's a start." He swallowed noisily. "From here on out we're going to be spending a lot more time together."

Billy put on a face of mock horror. "Man, maybe I was better off before."

Linda ignored this remark and began tidying up the table. "We've never had a month off, so we'd better make the most of it. Let's see if we can get you a few days off school for a family vacation."

"A vacation, eh?" said Billy. "You guys getting busted is going to work out in my favor." He was glad to get out of school and finally have some quality time with his parents. Still, he was a little disappointed to be leaving AFMECopolis so soon. He wanted to stay and find out more about creatches and being an Affy.

"Come on," Jim said as he rose from the table. "Let's blow this Popsicle stand."

They all got up, bused their trays, and headed back to pick up the van. Orzamo trotted along beside them.

Linda was now in plan-making mode and sounded genuinely happy about the prospect of having some time off. "What do you say we go see Gramma? Not today. Tomorrow. Once we get home and rest up a bit. She's got stories that'll make your head spin."

When they got back to the docking platform, Gordy came running out in a state of minor panic, his parrot creature yowling with displeasure.

"*There* you are, Mr. Clikk! Mr. Vriffnee needs to talk to you. Says it's urgent. Is there a problem with your viddy-fone or something?"

Jim wore a confused expression as he fished his viddy-fone out of his pocket. "No, Gordy. But we're on involun—on vacation right now. I switched it off."

"Well, you'd best switch it back on!" Gordy shouted as he dashed off to get the van, his parrot flapping madly to keep up with him.

TEEP

Mr. Vriffnee's voice came blasting out of the viddy-fone the moment Jim popped it open. The words were indistinct, but Billy could tell something big was going on. Jim could hardly get a word in.

"I'm sorry, Mr. Vriffnee, but I thought . . . Of course, Mr. Vriffnee . . . Yes, but . . . Certainly. . . . Certainly. . . . The Taj Mahal? Wow. . . . Yes, Mr. Vriffnee. . . . Thank you, Mr.

Vriffnee. . . . We won't let you down. . . . Absolutely. We'll report in as soon as we get there."

TEEP

"Gordy!" Jim called out as soon as he shut the viddy-fone off. "Better get the van loaded up for a ground-creatch operation. Weapons, ammo, and the full range of tranquilizers."

"I'm on it, Mr. Clikk!"

Jim turned to Billy with a tired smile. "Vacation's over, son. Skeeter gig. In India."

CHAPTER 11

"What is today," Jim asked as he revved the engine, "Thursday?"

Linda chuckled. "No, honey. It's Saturday."

They were back on the little island of stone where they'd first arrived. Jim pulled a few knobs on the dashboard and the van slowly rose into the air.

"Saturday? Already? Oh well, at least we won't have to come up with an excuse for Billy not being in school today."

"Wait a minute," Billy said. "You mean I'm coming *with* you guys? I thought Mr. Vriffnee said—"

"He changed his mind, son," Jim said. "We've got to be in India ASAP. No time for pit stops back in Piffling."

I'm going to India, thought Billy. *How much weirder is this day going to get?* "All right, so . . . what exactly are we going to be doing in India?"

"*We,*" Linda said, glancing at Billy to make sure he understood that *we* referred only to his parents, "will be handling a code-red invasive creatch operation. *You* will be watching from a safe distance."

Safe distance? Billy didn't like this.

"But Mom, this is the perfect chance for me to begin my Affy training," he said. "That Ana girl was battling creatches when she was nine years old. I'm twelve already, and I'll be thirteen before the end of the year. . . ."

"Now, hang on, son," said Jim. "Ana didn't go on a creatch op the day after she was brought to AFMECopolis. She was younger than you, sure, but she went through months of prep before they decided she was ready to get some experience in the field."

"Come on, Dad, you've got to at least let me help."

"Oh, we'll find something for you to do, don't worry. But you're not going to go head to head with a creatch on your first day out."

"I'm not asking to go head to head. But I want to be close enough to *see* the thing at least."

"Just . . . be patient, kiddo. You'll get your chance to see a creach once you've passed the exams. A year or two from now, tops."

"A *year* or two?" said Billy. "That's *ages*."

"Take it easy, darling," said Linda. "I was just as anxious to see a creach when I was your age. But you've got to take things one step at a time."

Billy kept quiet for a minute or two. He was frustrated but he hadn't given up yet.

Maybe the creach will come out in the open. Or they'll change their minds. I've gotta sneak a peek somehow. . . .

He changed his tone of voice to sound as if he'd accepted their decision but simply wanted more information. "So what kind of creach are you going to be dealing with?"

"An orf," Jim said. "A type of ground creach. One of them has taken up residence in the Taj Mahal. As you can imagine, the local authorities aren't too tickled about it."

"This one will be tricky," said Linda. "Getting rid of the orf without damaging the Taj is going to be a *very* delicate procedure."

"A creach in the Taj Mahal," said Billy. "Man, this must be all over the news and everything."

"Actually, they've managed to keep it under wraps. Most governments have people in their own media who understand the importance of secrecy in these matters. So far as the world is concerned, the Taj is temporarily closed due to a water-main break."

"I get it. So you two are going to go into the Taj Mahal and kill this orf?"

"Oh, we won't kill it if we don't have to," Linda said. "Just knock it out. We've got an assortment of tranquilizers that usually do the job. Once the creatch is unconscious, it's simply a matter of getting it back to creatch-controlled territory."

"What's an orf look like?"

"There's a book up there in that locker in front of you," Linda said. *"The AFMEC Guide to Ground Creatches.* See it?"

Billy looked up, opened the locker above his head, and found a massive black book among many others on a shelf.

"Look under *O.* There should be a picture there."

Billy flipped through the book, past illustrations of long-necked creatches, hundred-legged creatches, and creatches with heads where their navels ought to be. He came at last to a single page relating to orfs.

An illustration carefully rendered in the manner of nineteenth-century engravings depicted a black, furry beast with dozens of hairy tentacles. The silhouette of a man drawn next to it showed that the orf was roughly five times as large as a human: big enough, Billy imagined, to eat the man and still have room for more.

Billy read through the paragraphs beneath the illustration and soon came to the conclusion that Affys didn't know as much about these orfs as they would like.

DIET: Further study needed. Some researchers have suggested a fondness for the flesh of goats, based on carcasses found during cleanup operations. Teeth are large, tightly packed, and capable of tearing through flesh with astonishing speed. One agent, who lost the better part of his left leg to an orf, reported that the limb was severed and swallowed in under a second. Evidence suggests, however, that orfs prefer swallowing their prey whole.

LANGUAGE COMPREHENSION: None. Rumors persist of orfs that can be trained to understand simple commands, but there is no hard evidence of this.

MOVEMENT: Orfs move primarily by burrowing through the earth using claws that project from their tentacles, then retract when not in use. On rare occasions they have been seen moving overland at speeds in excess of forty miles per hour, but, like most ground creatches, they prefer to stay out of sunlight whenever possible.

DEFENSES: Orf saliva is a green gelatinous substance that is believed to induce drowsiness in humans after prolonged exposure. Orfs are said to be capable of using their tentacles to throw objects with startling accuracy. Orf tentacles can also take hold of prey and constrict with lethal force; studies of mangled goat flesh suggest tentacles are capable of strangling prey at pressures up to seven tons per square foot.

WEAKNESSES: Poorly understood.

SUGGESTED CREATCH OP TECHNIQUES: Unclear. Some agents have reported success with tranquilizers; others have found them entirely ineffective. Nets and traps have had limited success. Agents are urged to exercise extreme caution. Though few agents have been killed by orfs, those who have are thought to have died slowly and in almost unimaginable pain.

"Wow," said Billy. "These orfs are heavy-duty."

"Yes," said Linda. "Which is all the more reason why you need to keep a safe distance. An orf could eat five boys your age without even thinking about it. We've got protective gear, so you don't have to worry about us. But trust me, you're going to want to be as far away from this thing as you can get."

I'll be the judge of that, thought Billy.

Several hours later they landed in Agra—or rather, on a dusty road outside Agra, where they raised a fuss among a herd of cows but otherwise didn't attract much attention.

Linda consulted a map while his father steered the BUGZ-B-GON van through narrow lanes past towering Hindu temples and women carrying bronze-colored pitchers of water on their heads. There were white-bearded beggars, carpet vendors, and men sitting down for a shave right on the side of the road. One old turbaned man was selling tea in tiny clay cups that customers disposed of by simply smashing them on the ground.

Billy had never seen anything like India, that was for sure. Or smelled anything like it either. Every time he inhaled he caught different scents mixed together: curry, manure, flowers, exhaust fumes, and always something deep-fried and spicy-smelling from food stalls along the road.

They arrived in downtown Agra and rumbled onto a road that followed a wide, slow-moving river on their left. As they inched their way down the traffic-clogged street, Billy caught his first glimpse of the Taj Mahal, its domes and minarets tinged pink by the morning sunlight. A flock of birds no larger than specks passed before one of its archways, serving as a crude measure of how massive the building really was. But it wasn't the size of the Taj Mahal that impressed Billy. It was the perfection of it: the smooth surfaces, the flawless symmetry.

Billy tried to imagine the hairy, black-tentacled beast from *The AFMEC Guide to Ground Creatches* lurking somewhere deep within the walls of this beautiful building. It was hard to picture.

Finally they reached the front gates, which were blocked by barricades and a small army of policemen. A mustached guard stepped to their window and Linda spoke to him in his own language, babbling on and on as if she were a native of India instead of Indiana.

"Your mom's a real whiz when it comes to Hindi," Jim said.

Linda said something that made the policeman hold his sides and laugh.

"So how many languages does Mom speak?"

"What, fluently?" His father made a face as if he was going to try to count, then just gave up. "Twenty. Thirty. I don't know. *Lots*. Lots and lots."

"So Mom's the brains of the operation," said Billy with a grin.

Jim laughed loudly. "Well, I'm no moron, kiddo. But, yes,

your mother's got me beat when it comes to languages and memorization. Me, I focus more on the hands-on stuff: repairs when equipment breaks down, that sort of thing. But that's not all I fix. Sometimes creatch ops don't go as smoothly as we'd like. I'm the guy who patches things up with the local authorities. With a place as revered as the Taj Mahal, I'll be working overtime to reassure folks that everything will turn out okay."

"So *will* everything turn out okay?"

"We haven't wrecked a Wonder of the World yet," said Jim with a chuckle. He was trying to sound casual, but Billy could tell his father was nervous. He had to be under a lot of pressure, trying to remove a creatch from such a famous piece of architecture.

The guard waved them past, and Jim parked the van inside the Taj Mahal compound. As they got out, Billy noticed that the BUGZ-B-GON logo had disappeared from the exterior of the van. In its place was Hindi lettering that matched what he'd seen on signs and shop windows as they came into town.

"Local-color camouflage," Jim explained. "You should see what the van looks like when we're in the Caribbean."

"Mr. and Mrs. Clikk!" Another mustached man—this one short, fat, and nervous-looking—trotted across the courtyard to greet them. "Thank you for coming here on such short notice. I am Ravi Goswami, local Indo-AFMEC relations."

Jim and Ravi shook hands so hard it looked as if they might break something. "Glad to meet you, Ravi. And call me Jim, why don't you, since we've got two Mr. Clikks here today. Meet Billy."

Billy immediately found his hand snapped into Ravi's. "Ah, this must be your son. Carrying on the family business, are you?" Ravi's voice went up and down like a children's song. "Maybe you can help us with this pesky creatch of ours." He meant it as a joke, but judging from the panicked expression on his face, Billy figured he wouldn't turn down help from anyone at this point, twelve-year-olds included.

Jim grinned and waved a hand toward Linda. "Ravi, you already know my wife, don't you?"

"Ah yes, Mrs. Clikk," Ravi said, shaking Linda's hand no less forcefully than he had the others'. "We are still indebted to you for your help with those dreadful naggatroffs in Calcutta two summers ago."

Linda smiled modestly. "You had the situation pretty well under control, Ravi."

"Ha!" Ravi pulled a handkerchief from his pocket and mopped his brow. "Half the population would have been eaten alive if not for you." He turned to Billy. "Thank heavens your mother was able to dispense with those naggatroffs before they got to the outskirts of the city, before anyone even saw them. The people of Calcutta will never know how lucky they are."

"What are naggatroffs?" asked Billy.

"You don't want to know, my boy," said Ravi, scrunching his face up into a look of pure revulsion. "One-third serpent. One-third hippopotamus. One-third enormous, angry lobster. If I never see another it will be too soon."

Billy's parents nodded sympathetically.

"I was so impressed with how your mother handled those wretched beasts," Ravi continued, "that I told Mr. Vriffnee: 'For the Taj Mahal it must be the Clikks and no one else.' He was strangely resistant to the idea of sending you, actually. . . ."

Jim clapped his hands and began to roll up his sleeves. "Well, Ravi, sounds like you've got an orf around here with our name on it."

"Of course, of course. Step right this way."

They walked through a red sandstone gateway, Orzamo trotting along beside them, and entered a vast, carefully manicured garden on the other side. Beyond the garden, mirrored in a long shallow pool of water, was the Taj Mahal. Billy had seen photographs of it dozens of times, but it still made his jaw drop.

"Wow," he said.

It stood on a vast platform with interlocking squares like a gigantic chessboard. Four slender minarets—one at each corner of the platform—soared well over a hundred feet into the air; the pinkish tinge Billy had seen earlier had now been cast off in favor of a shimmering yellow-white, the color of polished ivory.

"Wow," he said again.

The Taj Mahal was like a humongous jewel box, with at least half its surface chiseled into designs both delicate and startlingly precise: many-petaled flowers, gracefully curving vines, and inlaid stones of red and green. There were verses from the Koran surrounding every arched entranceway, so intricate and intertwined they looked more like illustrations than words. On top of it all was the huge onion-shaped dome, crowned by a brass finial that rose several more stories into the sky, glittering as it caught and reflected the morning sunlight.

Billy's parents weren't even looking at the Taj Mahal. Their attention was devoted to a series of black-and-white video monitors arranged on a folding table. Billy stuck his head between his parents' shoulders to see what was going on.

"Unfortunately," said Ravi, pointing to a monitor, "the cameras have not provided us with a direct view of the creatch. But here you can see a pile of bones from some animals he dragged in with him."

"Goat bones," said Billy.

"That's what it looks like," said his mother, nodding approvingly.

Billy's chest puffed out.

I could get pretty good at this. If I keep it up, maybe they'll let me go on the creatch op.

Linda pointed to a different monitor and turned her attention back to Ravi. "How about this hole here?"

Ravi winced. "That." He shook his head. "That is where the creatch has burrowed through the walls and made a home for itself. The cost of repairs . . ." He rolled his eyes and made a fluttering gesture with his hands: money scattering to the winds. ". . . I don't even want to *think* about it."

Jim turned to Linda. "Well?"

Billy watched his mother's face as she turned from one monitor to another. She put a finger to her lips and adjusted her glasses. Then she pulled a pad of paper from her back pocket and began scribbling on it like a doctor writing a prescription.

"We'll start with a phased-in program of tranquilizers. Floxodril to begin with: three canisters every ten minutes for two hours. If that doesn't work, we'll move up to gremadril. Then borradril."

"Uh, Mom," said Billy. "That book said tranquilizers don't work with orfs."

Linda turned to Billy. For some reason she looked less impressed with Billy's show of knowledge this time. She actually looked a little irritated. "No, Billy. It says that some Affys have reported success with tranquilizers, while others haven't. That doesn't mean we shouldn't begin by giving them a try."

I'm only trying to help. Jeez.

"Look, son," said Jim, "we appreciate your enthusiasm. Really we do. But your mother knows a wee bit more about creach battling than you do, don't you think?" He chuckled, but the message was clear: Zip it, young man.

Billy sighed.

Jim turned to Ravi and patted him on the back. "Leave this to us, Ravi. The Taj Mahal will be de-creatched by sundown." Ravi's eyes lit up. "Tomorrow afternoon at the latest." Ravi clearly preferred the earlier estimate, but he smiled and bowed anyway.

"Thank you, Mr. and Mrs. Clikk," he said, saluting them as if they were generals. "All of India is counting on you." He walked away slowly, somehow looking worried even from behind.

"All right, Billy boy," Jim said, "time for Mom and Dad to go to work."

Linda handed Billy a small device about the size and shape of a ballpoint pen. There were two buttons on the side: one black, one red. "Your father and I are going to set up an imperm barricade. It's a sort of force field that prevents anyone from entering or leaving the scene of a creach op. If you need us, press the red button. That'll send us a signal and we'll be out here as soon as we can."

"The *red* button," Jim said, raising his index finger. "Not the black one."

Billy leaned over and whispered conspiratorially. "Psst . . . Dad, come on. Help me out here. Let me come along. I'll be careful."

Jim Clikk refused to play the game. He spoke loudly and clearly: "I'm sorry, Billy. Your mother and I are in agreement. We're not talking about skateboards and mountain bikes here. This is dangerous stuff. You're only twelve years old. I didn't take part in *my* first creach op until I was seventeen."

Billy turned to his mother. "Please, Mom. Just let me help you set up your equipment."

"Sorry, Billy. These devices are extremely dangerous in inexperienced hands. Trust us. This is for your own good. There'll be plenty of work for you to do later when the cleanup operations begin."

"Cleanup operations?" Billy groaned. "I've heard about

that. It's what they make Affys do when they get demoted. What is it, like a mop and a bucket?"

"You've got to start somewhere, son," said Jim. "Your mother and I did a lot of mopping up before we took part in any creatch ops. Your time will come. Be patient. Now run along and have fun."

I can't believe this. They're treating me like a five-year-old.

Jim patted Orzamo on her furry terrier head. "Show Billy some of your tricks, Orzy. And I don't mean rolling over and playing dead." Jim gave Billy a wink.

Linda mussed Billy's hair. "Don't take it too hard. There'll be plenty of time for creatch battling when you're older. Why, I wouldn't be surprised if you were authorized as a creatch op assistant by this time next year."

Billy briefly considered a variety of things he could say that might help him get his way. The expressions on his parents' faces seemed to shoot the words down before he even said them.

Forget it. They're not going to budge on this. Maybe I'll get a chance later on. Or maybe . . .

. . . a chance will present itself.

Billy nodded and played the obedient son. "Okay. Let me know if you need anything."

"That's the spirit," said Jim, giving Billy a soft punch in the arm. "Get to know Ravi, why don't you? I've heard he makes a mean cup of chai. It's half the reason we accepted this job." Another Jim Clikk wink.

The day crawled by. At first Billy had fun playing with Orzamo. She was able to do all kinds of amazing things: scale walls like a spider, change the color of her fur, breathe puffs of smoke. But Billy's eyes kept returning to the Taj Mahal, where his parents were lugging various pieces of equipment they'd pulled from the van: long harpoon-shaped weapons with flashing lights on the sides, metallic contraptions covered with dozens of spindly mechanical limbs, and one thing that looked like a cast-iron lawn mower with a satellite dish attached.

After about half an hour Billy saw his parents set up a circle of red poles in the gardens around the Taj Mahal, one every twenty or thirty feet. Linda waved and called out to Billy: "We're switching on the barricade now, Billy." A moment later there was a brief flash of electricity, like lightning coming from the ground instead of the sky. "Don't go anywhere near the red poles. Those are the barricade markers. If you try to cross the barricade . . ." She paused as she considered which words to use. "Well, at best you'll look pretty stupid. At worst, you'll end up flat on your back in the nearest hospital." She waved once more and disappeared through one of the arched entrances.

That was the last Billy saw of his parents for several hours. They stayed inside the Taj Mahal, and anyone looking at the building from the outside would never have suspected that anything unusual was going on within.

There were sounds, though. Rattling noises. Low electric hums that rose and fell like ambulance sirens. Smells, too: pungent, smoky odors that drifted across the gardens and made Billy more curious than ever. At one point a tremendously loud bang echoed across the gardens, sending birds whirling into the sky.

"What are they *doing* in there?"

Orzamo made a tired bleating sound, suggesting it was of very little interest to her. She tried to get Billy's attention by causing a pebble to levitate.

"Cool," said Billy. But he wasn't really focusing on Orzamo. He was thinking of the Taj Mahal. Wishing he could be on the inside, battling the orf with his parents.

Ravi came by and invited Billy to join him for a cup of chai in his tent. Billy accepted and killed some time shaded from the worst of the afternoon sun, sipping the super-sugary tea and listening to Ravi tell tales of what must have been every creach op on the subcontinent for the last five centuries.

Between stories, Ravi mentioned something he'd once heard.

"It is said that all the orfs in India have a hidden Achilles' heel. A weakness that, if properly exploited, is guaranteed to kill them."

Billy nearly spilled his chai. This was important.

"Where is it?"

"Right here." Ravi raised his upper lip and pointed to a spot at the center of his gum line.

"The gums? Just above the front teeth?"

"That's right. You need only tap that spot with your pinky and an Indian orf will fall unconscious, straightaway."

"You're kidding. How is that possible?"

"Well, it makes quite a lot of sense when you think about it," said Ravi. "It's a part of the body that is only rarely exposed. Evolution evidently saw no need to provide much protection for it."

Billy examined Ravi's face. This was no joke: he looked as if he really believed what he was saying.

"How do you know all this stuff, Ravi? Are you an expert on creatches or something?"

"Oh no," said Ravi with a laugh and a wave of his hand. "I'm no expert. But my grandfather knew a man whose friend was once an Affy-in-training. He never made it to full Affy status, mind you. But he learned a thing or two before he returned to normal society, I can tell you that."

Billy thought this over. The guy had been an AFMEC insider: a pretty reliable source of info.

"The gums," said Billy.

"Yes, yes: the gums. But you've got to hit them directly in the right spot. An inch too far to the left or right and all your efforts will be in vain. Not only that"—Ravi raised his eyebrows mischievously—"but you'll also be eaten. For anyone so foolhardy as to try jabbing an orf in the gums *deserves* to be eaten, don't you think?"

Ravi laughed loud and long, his belly shaking in big, quivering waves. When he had recuperated from the fit of giggles that followed, he immediately launched into another tale.

Billy had stopped listening, though. He was thinking about the orf. About the Achilles' heel. And about his mom and dad—wondering if they knew about the story.

I'll bet they don't. It wasn't in the book. It was probably something this Affy-in-training guy figured out on his own. It could be a shortcut to defeating the orf.

Ravi kept talking. Billy kept thinking.

I mean, the pinky-tapping bit is ridiculous. But what if you had a weapon? What if you were able to fire something into that spot?

As Ravi's stories continued unabated, Billy convinced himself that he was on to something.

I've got to give it a try. If I could defeat the orf on my own, they'd make me an Affy right away. They did it for that Ana girl. They'd have to do it for me. They'd have no choice.

Billy waited until Ravi had finished his latest tale before rising and excusing himself. "Thanks for the chai, Ravi. It was great."

"You're more than welcome, my dear boy," said Ravi as Billy reemerged into the late-afternoon sun. "Next time I'll tell you about the flame-throwing floggle-bats of Bombay. They made the naggatroffs seem like dinner party guests."

Billy spent the rest of the day coming up with a plan.

Mom and Dad aren't going to work all night. No way. Not after all that time in the Philippines. They're going to need sleep. And when they do . . .

Noises and smells continued to come from the Taj Mahal, but Billy saw nothing of his parents until sundown, when they trudged out into the garden, dirty and exhausted. Their jumpsuits were covered with green stains.

"We nearly had him there, Linda," said Jim. "When you fired the magnetic-fusion plasmatron at him and I got the graggler net around one of his tentacles . . ."

"What's a plasmatron?" asked Billy.

"A very handy piece of hardware," said Jim. "It shoots a bolt of purple plasma that inflicts serious pain with every direct hit. Five good blasts and most creatches are out cold. It's about this big"—he set his hands three feet apart—"with a plasma receptacle here, and—"

"I thought for *sure* the borradril would do the job," said Linda as she tugged a glove off and threw it on the ground. She seemed preoccupied with the mission and not in the mood to hear Billy's father sing the praises of their equipment.

She doesn't know about the Achilles' heel, thought Billy. *Otherwise they'd have defeated the orf by now.*

"Don't worry, honey," said Jim. "We'll get him. We've got all day tomorrow."

"Something really strange is going on," said Linda. "Did you see his eyes? Not the right color. It's like there's a temporary chemical imbalance or something. I've seen it somewhere before, but I can't remember where. . . ."

"How about this, honey. We'll have some dinner. Get Billy set up for bed. Then we'll put in one more shift, and if things don't go our way, we'll have a fresh go at it tomorrow morning. We've got loads of options left. There is the ribblavator. The ultrasonic pulse-darts. And we haven't even *touched* the semi-lethal weaponry yet."

Linda coughed, took a deep breath, then reached down and picked up her glove. "Okay."

One more shift, thought Billy, *and they'll have a fresh go at it tomorrow morning. One more shift. A few more hours at most. Then they'll go to sleep.*

They all sat down for a quick meal of tandoori lamb and freshly baked flatbread, then retired to a tent set up for them by Ravi Goswami and his men. As soon as Billy was safely in his sleeping bag, Jim and Linda went back to the Taj Mahal for another round with the orf.

Several hours later they returned. They exchanged a few whispered words about how poorly their second shift had gone, changed clothes, and went to sleep. The tent became very, very quiet.

Billy was wide awake.

He had, in fact, never really gone to sleep in the first place.

He waited until his parents were snoring, then slipped out of his sleeping bag, quietly unzipped the tent, and crept out into the cool night air.

Am I really going to do this?

He had it all worked out: he'd sneak into the Taj Mahal, snag one of Mom and Dad's weapons, find the orf, and shoot it right in the gums. If Ravi was right about the whole Achilles' heel thing, the orf would keel over, end of story. If he was wrong . . . well, the orf was bound to be knocked out for a minute or two. Billy could escape and sneak back to the tent. Tomorrow morning his parents would be none the wiser.

And who were *they* to boss him around, anyway? They'd been absentee parents all his life. They had no right to tell him what to do and what not to do. Where had they been when he'd won first prize at the X-Sports Challenge in front of Dave's Cycle and Fitness? Or when he and Nathan had jumped off the Flawatamee Bridge using their own homemade bungee? They hadn't been in Piffling, that was for sure. And even if they had been, come on. His parents were out there risking their lives every day. Why shouldn't he take those same chances?

Billy dropped to his hands and knees and began crawling in the direction of the Taj Mahal.

CHAPTER 12

Keeping low to the ground in case any guards were watching, Billy continued to make his way toward the Taj Mahal, which took on a strange blue glow in the moonlight: its minarets stately and sparkling, its archways shadowy and mysterious.

Man, I wish Nathan could see me now. Or even better, a few minutes from now, after I've got my hands on one of those weapons. Too bad I can't get someone to take a picture.

He had only covered a few yards when he heard something.

What the—

He stopped.

Footsteps made a soft *pat-pat-pat*ting sound some ten or twenty yards ahead of him. He rolled under a nearby hedge just in time to avoid being seen by one of Ravi's men, a guard on patrol. He was tall and muscular, wearing a gold-braided cap and an olive green uniform. He had a walkie-talkie in his hand and what looked to be a gun in a holster attached to his belt.

Jeez, thought Billy. *I've got to be more careful. I could blow my cover before I even get started.*

When the guard was a safe distance away, Billy cautiously resumed his crawl toward the Taj Mahal. He'd covered a good thirty yards when suddenly a second noise so faint it was barely audible came from somewhere behind him.

He stopped.

The sound stopped. Not that the night was entirely quiet. Far from it: crickets chirped in the hedges on either side of him, and cicadas droned somewhere in the distance. A breeze whistled through the trees, rustling leaves and causing branches to creak. But the sound he thought he'd heard—the sound of someone moving—had stopped.

He slowly turned his head and scanned the garden path behind him.

Nothing.

My mind's playing tricks on me.

He kept moving.

The sound resumed, louder than before.

He stopped again.

Silence.

Then . . .

. . . it started again.

Billy's heart was pounding. He broke into a sweat.

It's one of Ravi's men. He's been following me the whole time.

The sound was getting closer. It was almost right on top of him.

How am I going to explain this? He's going to wake up Mom and Dad and I'll be under surveillance for the rest of the—

Something brushed his leg.

Billy whirled around and found . . .

. . . a lizard. A big, yellow lizard.

"Orzamo!"

She was sitting there just a few feet away from him: eyes squinting, claws scratching against the concrete. Billy let out a long sigh of relief.

"Orzamo, you can't come with me. Go back to the tent." Billy made a shooing motion with his hands.

Orzamo puffed up her lower lip and shook her head. She was projecting a very different vibe from what Billy was used to: as if she knew she outranked him when it came to AFMEC affairs and could no longer be expected to just take his orders with a wag of her tail.

Billy made a short mouth fart.

"Oh, all right. But listen," he said. "You've gotta stay quiet. The whole time, no matter what. Deal?"

Orzamo growled and drew her mouth down at the corners. She carried her head high, and Billy sensed that he needed to start talking to her in a different way.

"Okay. Let's try this again." Billy ran a hand through his hair. "If you want to come with me, there's nothing I can do to stop you."

Orzamo widened her nostrils and produced a brief snort, as if Billy's statement went without saying. It suddenly dawned on Billy that Orzamo was the one calling the shots in this situation.

"You're not going to try to stop me, are you?"

Orzamo remained quiet. She had evidently not ruled out blowing the whistle on Billy.

"Oh, come on, Orzy. You wouldn't squeal on me. Would you?"

Still quiet.

Billy searched Orzamo's eyes, trying to understand what was going on behind them.

"You're on my side, Orzy. You've gotta be. I mean, you never approved of Mom and Dad leaving me home alone all the time, did you?"

Pieces were sliding together in Billy's mind: things Orzamo

had done—and hadn't done—from the moment he'd seen his parents on TV.

"You . . . wanted me to find out about AFMEC."

Orzamo glanced away. Billy knew he was on to something.

"I mean, maybe not consciously. You tried to stop me but . . . you didn't try as hard as you could have. You'd been against Mom and Dad keeping me in the dark all these years. So when the time came for me to have a chance at figuring everything out . . ."

Orzamo had turned back to face Billy. The faintest trace of a smile was forming on her lips.

". . . you let it happen."

Orzamo nodded ever so slightly, ever so slowly.

"Okay, Orzy. You let me make the phone call. You let me find out about AFMEC, and creatches, and everything else. The only reason I'm here where I am—doing what I'm doing—is because of you."

Orzamo glanced back toward the tent. Billy could see that she was torn between her orders from Mom and Dad and her devotion to Billy: not as a pet, but as a friend.

"I can't turn back now. I gotta go fight this orf. My mind's made up. So let's do it together, right now. You and me."

Orzamo stepped back and cocked her head, as if Billy had

gone one step too far. Her eyes were squinted almost to the point of being closed, and her brow was furrowed with indecision.

"Come on, Orzy. Please. We can do it. I know we can. And when we do, Mom and Dad'll be blown away. I mean, they'll be so impressed they'll wish they'd let us start battling creatches together ages ago."

Orzamo let out a long, low bleating sigh: a sound that indicated that—for the time being, anyway—Billy's persuasive powers had prevailed. She followed it up with a defiant snort, though, which Billy took as a warning not to push things too far.

"Thanks, Orzy," he said. "You and I are gonna make a great team. I know it."

Orzy rolled her eyes.

Billy smiled. It dawned on him that Orzy's coming after him was actually a stroke of good luck. Her demi-creatch powers were going to be a big help when it came to fighting the orf.

Billy took the lead and the two of them made their way toward one of the red poles outside the Taj Mahal: the imperm barricade. Billy had been thinking about this obstacle and had an idea for getting around it.

He stopped well short of the pole and pried a branch from a nearby bush. Reaching out his arm, he pointed the branch in the air near the pole. Nothing. He leaned forward, jabbing the branch beyond the red pole to the other side. Nothing.

"Hm. Some barricade."

But when Billy jabbed the branch just a little farther he felt it hit something. There wasn't a sound, but the branch stopped moving forward, as if he were jabbing it into a wall. And yet there *was* no wall: only air.

"Whoa."

Billy dropped the branch and carefully extended his arm in its place. Sure enough, his fingers splayed into the air, as if they were spreading out on a smooth, hard surface.

Yet he felt nothing against his skin but air.

"Awesome. It really *is* a force field."

He moved his hands across the strange invisible surface and watched with amazement as his fingers splayed again and again, making him look like some kind of pantomime artist. The imperm barricade was one of the coolest things he'd ever seen. Or *not* seen, that is.

Cool as it may have been, the barricade was something Billy needed to get past. He reached into his pocket and pulled out the penlike device his mother had given him earlier.

"*The red button*," his father had said. "*Not the black one.*"

"Hope I'm right about this." Billy clicked the black button, then put his hand out. To his great disappointment, the barrier was still there, just as solid as before.

"Maybe I need to double-click it."

He double-clicked the black button. But again his fingers splayed into the air, unable to budge even a fraction of an inch beyond the barricade. He tried everything: triple-clicking it, clicking it five times, ten times, twenty times. But no combination of clicks seemed to have any effect on the invisible barricade.

I should have known, Billy thought. *They wouldn't give me the power to shut down the barricade. Why would they?*

He was playing around with the idea of digging a hole underneath the barricade—something that would take many more hours than he had available—when it occurred to him that there was one thing he hadn't tried.

He pushed the black button down and held it down. Then he carefully extended his arm until the tip of the pen was close enough to reach the invisible barrier.

When it reached the imperm barricade, a tiny blue spark shot out from the tip of the device, followed by another, and another. Finally there were so many sparks shooting out, it looked as if the pen was creating a glowing blue splotch in midair.

Billy pulled the pen back and found to his astonishment

that the splotch stayed right where it was. It was if he had drawn on the surface of the invisible barrier with glowing blue ink. It slowly lost its luminescence, though, and within several seconds it was gone.

Billy looked behind him to see if any guards might be alerted to his presence. Fortunately all the guards were far enough away that even if they looked in his direction, their view would be blocked by a nearby hedge.

He pushed the black button again and extended the pen to where it had been before. This time he moved it: sure enough, a glowing blue line formed in the air. He moved the pen around until he had drawn a neat little circle in the air, then quickly stuck his hand into the middle of the circle.

It went through.

Yes!

As the circle vanished, Billy pulled his hand back out. When he reached back to the same spot a second later, the barrier was whole again.

So that's it, he thought. *A pen for "drawing" a temporary passageway through the barricade. Perfect!*

He drew another circle and counted the seconds it took for the line to disappear.

Seven . . . eight . . . nine . . . that's it.

"Ten seconds," he whispered to Orzamo. "We've gotta move fast."

Billy checked one more time for guards.

Oh, you've gotta be kidding me.

One of the guards—a big, burly one with glasses and a handlebar mustache—was heading straight toward him. There was still enough of the hedge in the way to keep Billy hidden, but with every step the guard took Billy's cover grew smaller.

"All right, Orzy," Billy whispered. "It's now or never."

He pushed the black button, drew a large circle in the air—slightly larger than a garbage can lid—and jumped through as soon as it was complete.

"Now, Orz!" he whispered as loudly as he dared.

Orzamo hesitated. The circle was already starting to disappear.

"Now!"

Orzamo leaped through the hole a second before it vanished. Billy grabbed her and rolled under a hedge on the other side of the barricade.

The guard stopped and looked around. He said something in Hindi and pointed a flashlight in their direction. Billy held his breath. So did Orzamo. For a good thirty seconds there was nothing but the sound of crickets.

"Hmf," grunted the guard after a moment, and continued on his rounds.

That was close, thought Billy. *But we're past the barricade now. With any luck that'll be the last guard we see until we come back out.*

Billy and Orzamo stayed under the hedge for a couple of minutes, breathing deeply, waiting. Then they continued on their path to the Taj. Ducking in and out of shadows, checking every minute or two to make sure they weren't being watched, they soon arrived at one of the huge arched entrances.

The interior of the Taj was cold and dark. Moonlight poured in through the carved marble latticework of one of the entranceways, casting spidery shadows on the floor. In the few spots where light hit the walls, exquisite floral designs crafted from inlaid stones—agate and lapis lazuli—glittered like jewels.

It was dead silent.

Billy's eyes immediately fell on a large tool kit set against one of the walls.

Bingo, he thought. *Creatch-battling stuff.*

He tiptoed over and read the words on the outside of the case:

MAGNETIC-FUSION PLASMATRON
MODEL NO. 5560-XQ7

"Dad mentioned this. One of the nonlethal weapons. Still, if I pop the orf a good one in the gums with this, it's bound to do *something.*"

Billy tried to open the case. No luck: it was held shut by a heavy padlock.

"Orzamo," Billy whispered. "Any idea how to open this thing?"

Orzamo looked nervous, as if this was breaking one rule too many.

"Come on, Orzy. If we're going to sneak down to go after that orf, we've gotta have a weapon."

Orzamo groaned a bit, cast her eyes to the heavens, then placed her jaws gingerly around the edges of the padlock. She paused, twisted her neck, and . . .

K'CHIK

The padlock popped open.

"Wow," said Billy. "You're good at that."

Orzamo winked and cocked her head back proudly.

Billy opened the tool kit. Most of the space inside was occupied by a device that looked an awful lot like one of those oversized plastic toy pistols that shoot water by the gallon. It was much more sleek and polished, though, as if composed of the carbon fiber material used to make stealth bombers.

Billy picked it up. It was surprisingly light. There were several handles and a spherical container near the front filled with a purplish liquid that sloshed around as he turned it over in his hands.

"What does it do?"

Orzamo shook her head. She looked even more nervous than before.

Billy raised it to eye level and tried to get a feel for how to take aim with it. It was tipped with a small cylindrical tube and a strange dispenser that looked like the spout of a watering can.

"Only one way to find out."

He pointed it at the floor and cautiously pulled the trigger.

VOOOOSH!

A bolt of purple fire shot out and ricocheted around the interior of the Taj like a miniature comet. Billy ducked, praying no one would see it from the outside. A few seconds later the fire bolt finally dissipated, and Billy inspected the spots where it had hit the floor and walls. There were some minor singes, but nothing serious. He figured it was unwise to try a second test shot.

"This is just the thing we need," he said as he tucked it under his arm. "One blast in the gums from *this* baby and that orf will be out cold."

Orzamo sighed. Still, she didn't seem to object to having a means of self-defense.

"Okay, now we've got to find the hole," said Billy. "The one Ravi pointed to on the video monitor."

They crept from one wall to another, finding ornamented surfaces wherever they turned, each with its own Arabic calligraphy, its own red and green flowers of inlaid stone. A chill ran down Billy's neck, and he had the sensation of being alone in a cemetery after sundown. The Taj was, after all, a mausoleum, and in the dead of night it was no longer the photogenic tourist destination it had been in the daytime. It was more like a chilly, sinister crypt.

Then, deep in one of the darkest shadows, they came upon the hole. It was four feet wide and five feet tall. Billy recalled the size of the orf from the illustration he'd seen.

It must be able to compress its body to move through tight passages.

The hole had been burrowed through a spot where the walls met the floor. Its edges were jagged, with tiny cracks extending several feet into the ornate surfaces surrounding it. Ravi was right: this hole would cost a small fortune to repair.

Billy turned his attention to the floor. It was covered with globs of green gunk—orf saliva, Billy assumed—and chewed-up goat bones. Using the tip of the plasmatron, he poked at a bit of the goo. The shiny green mass quivered like a serving of Jell-O.

Yuck.

Billy recalled the description of orf saliva he'd read in the *Guide to Ground Creatches*: *". . . a green gelatinous substance that is believed to induce drowsiness in humans after prolonged exposure."*

He thought for a minute. *The key word is* prolonged. *Gotta get down there and get the job done as quickly as possible.*

Billy peered through the hole and into the passageway on the other side. It was black: pitch-black. He would be operating in complete darkness.

"A flashlight." He winced. "How could I forget?"

Without a second's hesitation, Orzamo leaped into the hole and vanished.

"Orzy!" Billy called out as loudly as he dared. "Come back here!" *Oh, great. Some buddy you turned out to be.*

Seconds later, Orzamo reappeared. Her horns were glowing pale orange, as if lit from within.

"Glowing horns, eh? Not bad, Orzy. Not bad at all."

Billy poked his head through the hole. Orzamo's horns provided just enough light to see by. Or enough to stumble by, anyway; they glowed so dimly that Billy couldn't see anything a foot or two beyond her head.

"Oh well," he whispered. "Better than nothing."

Orzamo growled at his lack of gratitude.

"I mean, *perfect*. Dim lighting's perfect," said Billy. "Attracts less attention."

Orzamo registered approval at this change in attitude.

"Okay, this is it," said Billy. "Orf time."

He swallowed hard and climbed into the hole.

CHAPTER 13

The floor of the passageway was steep: it descended into the ground at nearly a forty-five-degree angle. It was also covered in green slime, causing Billy to slip and fall at least a half dozen times. Orzamo and her glowing horns sometimes moved around a bend, leaving Billy lost in the blackness. Even with Orzamo in sight he had to feel his way forward like a blind man, occasionally planting his hand wrist-deep in goo before finding the rocky surface below.

This is really disgusting. Being an Affy definitely has its drawbacks.

They moved farther and farther down the passageway. Billy guessed that they were twenty or thirty feet below the Taj Mahal. As they progressed, it became warmer and more humid.

It was hard to breathe. There was also a strange odor in the air, as if they were crawling into the den of a huge wet cat.

Billy's heart, which had been beating fast to begin with, really started thumping. He gripped the plasmatron with one hand and ran the other through his hair. He was dripping with sweat.

They came to a spot where the passage opened up into a larger space. Apart from a few goo-covered bones on the floor in front of him, Billy could see nothing but blackness. He sensed the size of the space not with his eyes but with his ears: his movements echoed off distant walls, making him feel as if he were in a vast underground cathedral.

"Can you see anything, Orzy?"

Orzamo shook her head and sniffed the ground.

Billy started breathing through his mouth.

Maybe we should just turn around now, before it's too late.

Orzamo made a nervous whining sound and turned to Billy as if awaiting a change in plans. Billy stared back at Orzamo, wishing for a moment that she would make the decision for him.

No. Not yet. We've come this far. I've got to at least take a shot at the orf.

They began to inch their way forward into the blackness.

Billy thought he heard something breathing.

That's just Orzamo.

Something breathing, something breathing.

Or me.

He was so nervous now he really had no idea.

He stretched one hand out and forced himself to move forward.

That was when a pair of eyes opened in front of him.

Billy gasped.

His heart skipped a beat—or several beats—and then resumed pounding even faster than before. Sweat poured down his face, soaking his clothes. He halted in his tracks, standing absolutely still.

Eyes.

Orf eyes.

They were shiny and solid black, like the eyes of a rat. Only the pale reflection of Orzamo's glowing horns provided any evidence that they were there at all. Billy guessed they were no more than fifty feet away.

He raised the plasmatron and held it as steady as his shaking hands would allow.

Words began to pop into Billy's head, sentences he'd memorized from the guidebook: *"Teeth are large . . . tightly packed . . . capable of tearing through flesh with astonishing speed . . ."*

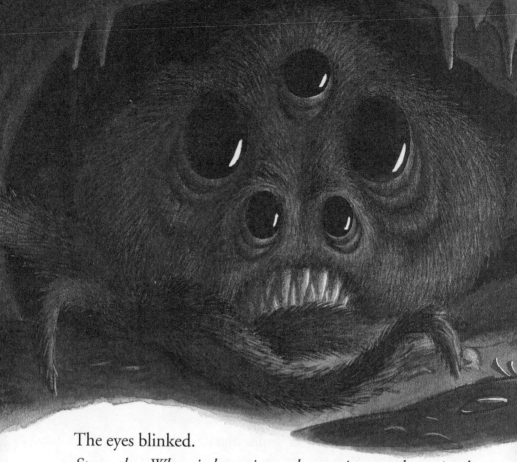

The eyes blinked.

Stay calm. When it bares its teeth, pop it a good one in the gums.

Two more eyes opened up, just below the first two. Then another, bringing the total to five.

"*One Affy . . . lost the better part of his left leg to an orf. . . . The limb was severed and swallowed in under a second. . . .*"

Billy gripped the plasmatron as tightly as he could.

KRRRRrrrrrrrr

A low, deep growling sound rumbled out of the darkness.

Billy thought he saw a glint of teeth.

Now!

Billy pulled the trigger.

VOOOOOOSH

A single blast of purple fire shot forward and vanished into the darkness, briefly illuminating the cave and its ceiling of stubby stalactites: the orf had dodged the fire bolt.

Billy fired again.

VOOOOOOSH!

This time the fire bolt struck the orf just above the eyes.

GAAAAAARRRRRR!

The sound was deafening, like a hundred lions roaring at once.

The orf was stunned. It backed away and clawed madly at the spot where the fire bolt had hit. It began to recover, though, much more quickly than Billy had anticipated. Within seconds its eyes were back open and it was moving closer. Billy wanted to take a third shot, but it was too late: the orf would be on top of him in no time.

Forget it. I missed my chance, I've gotta get out of here.

"Come on, Orzy!"

Billy gripped the plasmatron tightly and began scrambling back up the passageway. But before he'd covered even a few yards, something took hold of his leg.

No!

It snaked up around his belly.

Pulled him back.

Dragged him into the darkness.

"Orzamo!"

Something took hold of the plasmatron and yanked it out of his hands. He heard a clattering sound as it was tossed away.

Billy wasn't sure what happened next. His eyes might have been open. They might have been shut. It made no difference: there was nothing but blackness as he was dragged through passageway after passageway, his head smacking into rocks, bones, whatever lay in his path.

It's got me! It's gonna eat me!

Faster, faster, around corners, down tunnels so steep they were nearly vertical.

It can't eat me! I'm not a goat! The guidebook said it eats goats!

Down, down, deeper and deeper.

Finally he felt himself coming to a stop. The orf was dragging him more slowly. Its grip, however, hadn't changed in the least: five or six hairy limbs were locked around him, so tightly that his arms and legs were going numb.

Don't panic. Maybe it'll let me go when it sees I'm not a goat.

Billy bounced and skidded down one final passage. All at once his surroundings were made plain by bright white light: a kerosene lamp sat on the floor a yard or two from his head.

A kerosene lamp? What's that doing down here?

Billy was in a small cave, a rough circular space carved out of the earth somewhere deep underground. The floor was carpeted with bones and blobs of green goo. His heart was still pounding like crazy, and sweat covered his body, along with dirt and bone fragments and who knew what else.

Billy tried to turn his head to get a better view of his captor, but it was no use. All he could see was a tuft of black fur against his jaw, blurred by its proximity to his eyes. He could *feel* the orf, though. The limbs locked around him were warm and covered with scratchy hairs so coarse they stabbed like needles. The orf reeked, too. Like meat gone bad.

"Orzamo!" he whispered. "Come on, girl. Where are you?"

The yellow lizard was nowhere to be seen.

She bailed on me. I can't believe it.

All at once the orf released Billy, allowing him to roll across the floor to the other side of the room.

KRRRRrrrrrrr

The orf growled: a rough, ragged sound, angry and tense.

Billy raised his head from the floor and got his first good look at the thing.

Every inch of it was alive with masses of quivering black fur. Its head and body were one and the same: a big lumpy orb of undulating hairiness. There were at least seven eyes, possibly more; Billy found it hard to make an accurate count under the circumstances. And there were legs—boy, were there ever legs. They projected from the orf's body on all sides, slithering and writhing, making it look like an enormous hairy octopus. Some of the legs were ten or twenty feet long. Maybe they were arms, actually. Maybe it didn't matter.

The orf trained its eyes on Billy and breathed loudly. Billy noticed a six-inch-wide bald spot where the plasmatron had struck. The flesh was bruised but otherwise unscathed.

This was not how Billy had seen things going. He wondered if he could reason with this thing. Right now, anything was worth a try.

"Look," he said, recalling that the guidebook hadn't entirely ruled out the possibility of orfs understanding English, "I, uh, mean you no harm."

It was a pretty ridiculous thing to say: he'd fired a weapon at the creature just a minute or two earlier. Obviously he'd meant the orf a great deal of harm. Now that he was defenseless, though, it was an even *more* ridiculous thing to say. The orf was as big as a Sherman tank, and any fool could see who was capable of harming whom. Still, it seemed like the right way to start things out.

"I'm just a kid. I'm not an Affy." But in spite of everything that had happened, he still wanted to be an Affy. He just hoped he'd live to have the chance.

KRRRRrrrrrrr

"Listen. You like goats, right?"

KRRRRrrrrrrrrrrr

"Well, look at me. I'm not a goat. . . ."

KRRRRrrrrrrrrrrrrrr

"I'm not even *close* to being a goat . . ."

KRRRRrrrrrrrrrrrrrrrrrr

". . . but I could *get* you some goats. Some nice, plump, juicy ones . . ."

KRRRRrrrrrrrrrrrrrrrrrrr

"I can't bring them to you, though, if you don't let me go."

KRRRRRrrrrrrrrrrrrrrrrrrrr

"So whaddya say?"

GAAAAAAAAAAARRRRRRR!

A hole opened below the orf's eyes, revealing an impossibly large set of teeth: dirty yellow, razor sharp, jutting out in every direction. A black tongue rolled around behind them, causing big globs of gooey green saliva to bubble out and ooze to the floor.

"Orzamo!" Billy hollered as loudly as he could.

Still no response. Wherever she was, it wasn't here.

Billy raised himself on his elbows and scooted as far away from the orf as he could. Sadly, this added only about an inch to the distance between the two of them, since Billy had been pretty much up against the wall to begin with.

Two hairy black arms crept across the floor toward his feet.

"Please . . . ," he said.

A third arm joined the first two, then a fourth and a fifth.

". . . if, if, if you let me go . . ."

The arms began to wind around Billy's feet.

". . . I'll bring you a dozen goats. *Two* dozen. I *swear*."

The arms began to drag Billy across the floor, straight toward the mouth.

"Nooooo!"

KRRRRRRRrrrrrrrr

Billy was now close enough for the green mouth goo to fall onto his legs in big wet globs. His heart was pounding so hard he thought it might explode.

"You don't want to eat me. *Really* you don't."

Blop. A melon-sized dollop of goo landed on Billy's thigh.

"I mean, look at me. *Very* little meat. All skin and b-bones."

Splop. Another one, right in the middle of his belly.

"Mostly bones, actually, hardly any skin . . ."

KRRRRRRRrrrrrrrr

The orf raised Billy's feet and guided them into its mouth. Billy felt the point of one of the orf's teeth jab into his ankle.

"P-poisonous bones!"

Soon nearly half of Billy's body was inside the orf's mouth. Everything from the waist down was past the orf's lips. The rest of Billy was suspended just a few feet above the cave's floor.

"Ch-choking hazard bones!"

Bones.

Bones. That's it!

Billy reached back, grabbed one of the chewed-in-half goat bones from the floor of the cave, and clenched it in both his fists, jagged edge down.

I've still got a chance! If I can just stab him in his weak spot . . .

He raised it in the air and brought it down into the orf's gums with all the strength he had, right in the spot Ravi had described.

KREEEEEEEEEEEEEeeeeeeeeeeee

The orf's squeal was so loud, Billy wished he could plug his ears. But that would mean letting go of the goat bone, and he wasn't about to do that.

GRRRAAAAAWWWW!

The orf roared and opened its mouth even wider. It was in pain, but it wasn't unconscious: not by a long shot.

"Fall asleep!" cried Billy. "You're supposed to fall asleep!"

Several more arms emerged, lunged forward, and snapped around Billy's neck.

"Glpff!"

He hadn't even had time to take a good, deep breath, and as of right now taking any breath at all was no longer an option.

Maybe I didn't stab him hard enough. I've gotta try again. . . .

He raised the bone high in the air and prepared to bring it down for a life-or-death blow.

SHUPP

SHUPP

SHUPP

Three more orf arms shot around his wrists. They constricted with skin-burning force, and the goat bone dropped to the ground somewhere behind Billy's head.

That's it, thought Billy. *I'm going into the mouth. It's all over now.*

The orf stuffed Billy all the way into its mouth and began to draw its jaws closed around him. Billy felt himself plunge into a pool of warm gooey saliva as the orf arms let go of his body and withdrew. He immediately braced his feet against two of the orf's enormous molars and dug his nails into its spongy gums. He was determined not to go down the throat.

I don't want to die!

I've gotta hold on. . . .

. . . Gotta just . . .

. . . hold on. . . .

All went black as the mouth shut completely, sealing Billy off from the light, from the cave, from the rest of the world.

CHAPTER 14

"What've you got in there?"

It was a voice coming from somewhere outside the orf.

There's someone out there! I'm saved!

Only a second or two had passed since Billy had been stuffed into the orf's mouth. He could barely breathe (the smell was *beyond* disgusting) and he couldn't see a thing, but at least he was still inside the orf's mouth and not down in its belly. Strangely enough, the orf wasn't even trying to swallow Billy. It was just holding him in its mouth.

"What is it?" the voice said.

Billy wrestled an arm free from the goo and tried to clean out his ears for a better listen.

"Come on. Show me. Open your mouth and show me."

KRRRRRRrrrrrrrr

Billy clamped his hands over his ears. The growl was a whole lot louder when heard from inside the orf's mouth.

"Now! Open your mouth and spit it out, or I'll . . ."

BLLLUUBBSHHHhhhhhh

The orf spat Billy onto the floor. He landed with a great big *splop*, his legs and arms flung out in all directions, feeling as if he were half buried in a pile of warm jellyfish. He opened his eyes and saw . . .

Twain.

Twain?

Yes, it was him: the leader of the AFMEC squadron that had crashed through Billy's bedroom window the night before. There he was, standing in the middle of the cave, looking as surprised to see Billy as Billy was to see him.

He spoke to the orf—in English—and the orf understood.

After a couple of sloppy attempts and a hard fall on his butt, Billy managed to stand up. He coughed and rubbed his eyes. "Mr. Twain?"

Normally Twain would have been the last person Billy wanted to see, but under the circumstances his sudden appearance on the scene was very welcome.

"Billy!" Twain leaned forward to get a better look at him. "Billy Clikk!"

Billy sat up and stole a glance at the orf. It was somehow less scary than it had been just seconds before. Its teeth were still just as sharp and glinting, and its eyes still bugged out as if preparing to pop from its head. But it was strangely calm and motionless, like a soldier awaiting orders.

"Don't worry, Billy." Twain crouched down on one knee. "The orf won't hurt you now. I'm in charge here."

Twain? In charge?

"Thanks," said Billy. "Another minute and I'd have been . . . dinner."

Twain was not smiling. "You'd better tell me what you're doing down here, Billy."

"Well, I, uh . . . you see, my parents were assigned to, um, de-creatch the Taj Mahal, and . . ."

"I know that, Billy. We're not talking about your parents. We're talking about you."

"Right." Billy coughed again. "I . . . wanted to do some creatch battling, but Mom and Dad wouldn't let me."

"So you snuck down on your own."

Billy examined Twain's face before answering. He didn't look angry. Just annoyed.

"Yeah. That's right."

"All by yourself?"

"Yeah," Billy said. As soon as he said it, he realized it wasn't true: Orzamo had come with him. But something told him not to correct himself just yet.

Twain's up to something. I need to keep him talking. . . .

Twain turned to the orf and spoke to it like a doctor talking to a patient. "Show me your gums. I think I saw a wound."

The orf obediently bared its teeth.

"Oh, boy. Someone gave you a nasty little cut here." Twain turned back to Billy. "And I think I know who that someone is."

"I was trying to knock him out. That's . . . that's what Affys *do*, right?"

Twain chuckled and shook his head, as if Billy had just made a very public display of his own ignorance. "You've got a lot to learn, Billy. Indian orfs don't suddenly keel over when you stab them in the gums. That's an old wives' tale."

Billy remained silent.

What's going on down here? Why is Twain so chummy with the monster?

Twain folded his arms and squinted at Billy. "You have a knack for getting yourself into trouble, little man. This midnight excursion of yours is going to . . . complicate things."

"So why are *you* down here, Mr. Twain? I thought my parents were handling this."

Twain paused for two full seconds. "I'm here to help, Billy. Mr. Vriffnee called me in as backup in case something went wrong."

If that were true, I'd have heard Mom and Dad talking about it. If I can keep him talking, maybe he'll slip up.

"Well, you sure know how to handle this orf. My parents were totally stumped. How did you manage to turn it into a trained monkey?"

Another pause. "I hate to break it to you, Billy, but a lot of things stump your mom and dad."

"Then why didn't Mr. Vriffnee put *you* in charge of this mission?"

"Enough questions. You're not even supposed to be down here, much less interrogating *me* about AFMEC decision making."

Twain turned to the orf. "Stay here."

Billy noticed that Twain's right hand was resting on a device attached to his belt: a little gray box with a single black button.

"Alert me if you detect any further intruders." The orf grunted obediently.

Twain must have planted this orf here, thought Billy. *But why would he want to cause damage to the Taj? It's got to be part of a bigger plan.*

Twain motioned to Billy: "Follow me."

Billy didn't want to cooperate, but he had to find out what was going on. Twain was shady, that much was obvious.

Twain led Billy through a tunnel to another cave, this one much larger than the first. There were crates and canisters and a table covered with papers. Twain tossed a towel to Billy and told him to sit on one of the crates.

Billy tried to wipe off some of the green goo. He was beginning to feel really drained: the slime was doing its thing.

"You're going to have to stay here," said Twain, "while I . . . figure out what to do with you."

Billy cleaned himself off as best he could while struggling to keep his eyes open. His brain was beginning to feel sluggish.

Maybe he's trying to loot the Taj. That doesn't . . . make sense, though. The Taj Mahal isn't filled with . . . valuable objects. The value is in the building itself. Even if you removed some of the ornamentation from the walls . . . you'd never . . . be able to get away with selling it.

Billy could see that Twain wasn't letting him go anywhere. He decided to risk another question. It was dangerous, but it would be worth it if Twain gave up some valuable information.

"So, Mr. Twain, why's the orf really here? You got some sort of grudge against the Taj Mahal?"

"Oh, I've got nothing against the Taj. My problem is strictly with AFMEC." Twain's eyes were filled with hatred, as if the very name of the organization made his blood boil.

In a flash, Twain lunged forward, grabbed Billy's forearm, and snapped a thick white bracelet around his wrist. The bracelet was heavy, as if packed with steel.

"Just in case you get any funny ideas."

Billy examined the bracelet. A feeling of dread overtook him.

What is this thing?

He swallowed hard. Twain was going to keep him prisoner down here indefinitely.

Something really bad is about to go down. I was better off inside the orf's mouth. . . .

"So what happens next, Mr. Twain? Sounds like you've got big plans." Billy was getting angry. If Twain had a problem with AFMEC, he had a problem with Billy's parents. And though his parents weren't perfect, Billy wasn't about to let anyone mess with them.

Twain turned to Billy and smiled. "Let's put it this way, Billy. I've got a score to settle with dear old AFMEC. And tonight that score gets settled."

Billy just glared. He had a really bad taste in his mouth and was no longer the least bit sleepy.

Twain paused and thought his words over.

"Well, *begins* to get settled, anyway. Look, why don't you just sit back and rest a little, Billy. You've seen enough action for one night, don't you think?"

Billy was shaking. He wasn't sure what Twain was up to, but he would *not* let him get away with it.

"Look, I'm not going anywhere, Mr. Twain. You might as well tell me what the scam is. What are you going to do with that orf?"

Twain leaned over until his face was directly in front of Billy's. He smiled. "I told you, no more questions. Now shut up and stay put."

Billy tried to jump to his feet.

FZZZIIIIIITCH!

An intense electrical shock crackled through him. Every nerve in his body exploded with pain. He collapsed to the floor, all elbows and knees.

"See what happens when you don't follow orders?" Twain said. "It's called a detention cuff, Billy. And as you've just discovered, this one is in good working order."

"You won't get away with this, Twain," croaked Billy. His throat burned from the electric shock. "My parents will find me, and when they do—"

"I'm sure they will, Billy," Twain interrupted, unconcerned with Billy's half-finished threat. "Don't worry, though. I'll be ready for them."

Twain regarded Billy for a moment longer, then turned and left.

CHAPTER 15

Billy lay flat on his back, head turned to one side. He was completely alone in the vast, shadowy cave. He became aware of how quiet it was: no insect noises, no footsteps, nothing. He didn't like it.

Billy considered trying to sit up but didn't want to risk another shock. He knew that Twain was some kind of double agent, pretending to be a good Affy while he was betraying the whole organization. What was he after? The world was turning out to be a whole lot more complicated than Billy had ever imagined. First AFMEC, and now something even darker, more secretive.

Billy's eyes swept the room until they fell upon the table and the papers stacked on top of it.

If I can just get a look at one of those pieces of paper . . .

He tried to get to his feet but got an even worse shock than the first time, though that hardly seemed possible. Again he collapsed to the floor. He lay there for several minutes, trying to think of a way to get to the table without frying himself in the process.

He tried moving his arms: *FZZZIIIIIITCH!*

"Ouch."

He tried moving his legs: *FZZZIIIIIITCH!*

"Ooooh."

Through sheer force of will, Billy eventually found that he was able to scoot himself across the floor on his back, one inch at a time. It hurt, sure, but incremental movements were the only option: crawling was way too painful, and walking was completely out of the question.

After about ten minutes he was close enough to grasp one of the table legs with his hand. He closed his eyes and shook it as hard as he could.

FZZZIIIIIITCH!

"Yoooowwwwch!"

He opened his eyes. Just as he'd hoped, the corner of one piece of paper was now hanging over the edge of the table. Not by much, though. It was going to take a lot of electric shocks to get that thing to drop to the floor.

If only I could just jump up and grab it. Grab every sheet of paper on the whole desk!

Fat chance. I can't even get up on my knees *with this stupid cuff on. A few more shocks and I'll be a dead man.*

He closed his eyes and dug his nails into the table leg, preparing himself for another dose of pain as he gave it another shake.

FZZZIIIIITCH!

"Nnnnngghh!"

He opened his eyes. Not bad: the piece of paper had slid a good half inch farther off the table. Billy's body was really aching now, but with any luck it would only take three or four more attempts. Okay, probably more like five.

"Gotta be tough. I can *do* this."

Billy had imagined his first creatch op as being more along the lines of a really excellent video game: snowboarding through the Himalayas, nailing mountain creatches right and left with a semiautomatic laser pistol. Getting barbecued by Twain's electrotherapy was *not* what he'd had in mind.

He closed his eyes again. Gritted his teeth. Gripped the table leg with all his might.

FZZZIIIIITCH!

"Aarrrrrnnggh!"

He opened his eyes. Disaster: the piece of paper had actually moved back up onto the table, leaving an agonizingly small corner visible from where Billy lay.

Billy was in so much pain he couldn't even manage his usual mouth fart. For a good minute or so he just lay there staring into space.

Forget this. I'm going to electrocute myself before I get hold of that stupid thing. Why did I ever think I could complete the mission by myself anyway? I must have been totally out of my mind.

But then Billy thought of Twain and his grudge against AFMEC. He didn't need to know all the details of Twain's scheme to realize it was a serious wack-job of a plan.

If he pulls this off, people are going to get hurt—maybe even killed—and I'll bet Mom and Dad are going to be among the casualties. Somebody's gotta stop this guy, and it's gonna have to be me.

Swallowing hard, he gripped the table leg as hard as he could and shook it with all his might.

FZZZIIIIIITCH!

"*Aaaaaannnnngghhfff!*"

fshup

Billy opened his eyes just in time to see the sheet of paper tilt like a seesaw and slip off the tabletop.

"Yes! *Yes!*"

He let out a long sigh of relief as the piece of paper floated to the floor of the cave. It landed just a foot or two from his right hand. Gritting his teeth to bear one last blast of electricity, he grabbed the paper and held it tight in his fist. A feeling of triumph swept over him, and he dropped his head to the floor in exhaustion.

As soon as he regained his energy, he opened his eyes and examined the piece of paper. It was a detailed drawing of a cluster of buildings. There were minarets, archways, and an onion-shaped dome, all rendered in scratchy white lines on flimsy blue paper: It was a blueprint of the Taj Mahal. There were notes about pressure points and structural support systems.

Twain's trying to find weaknesses in the buildings. He must want to destroy the Taj Mahal. But how? He said the score was being settled tonight. What if the orf is just providing cover?

Billy had another look at the blueprint.

This is all about the structure of the Taj Mahal. What's holding it together. How the minarets were designed to fall away from the building rather than toward it. How much of the walls needs to come down before the dome collapses.

Billy noticed one word repeated over and over again: *kirradril.*

Floxodril. Gremadril. Borradril. Mom mentioned those when she was talking about their first shift. What were they used for?

He racked his brain for a moment before coming up with the answer.

Tranquilizers. They were all tranquilizers. So kirradril must be another type of tranquilizer. Mom didn't mention it, though. Like it wasn't one she planned on using for this creatch op. Why not? Must be dangerous.

Then, from just a few yards away:

KRRRRRrrrrrrrrrrrrr

Billy stared in horror as a hairy black arm nudged its way through the entrance to the cave.

The orf was back.

CHAPTER 16

A second arm followed. Then a third, a fourth, a fifth.

Please tell me I'm not going to get eaten again.

The orf slid through the doorway and crept slowly across the floor.

Oh, I'm definitely *going to get eaten again. With this stupid detention cuff on I'm a sitting duck. . . .*

But the orf crept past him and found a spot to rest against one of the walls. It seemed to have lost its appetite. Its eyes were half closed, and there was something sluggish about the way it was moving.

Billy watched as the orf shut its eyes and groaned.

It's . . . in pain.

The orf opened its mouth and belched, long and loud:

a great cloud of greenish brown smoke blasted Billy in the face. It was truly the most horrible stench imaginable.

Ah, jeez. It's got indigestion, for crying out loud.

The orf belched again. This time a wet, gurgling noise accompanied the belch. The orf's eyes bugged out. Its arms made desperate circles in the air.

Oh no, this is worse than indigestion. It's going to throw up!

The orf whined loudly before grumbling, gagging, and coughing up a spectacularly large glob of green goo. The glob splapped onto the ground just inches from where Billy lay, big as a sack of potatoes. Bigger.

"Oh, I can*not* believe this," Billy said. "This is too gross for words."

Then, just when he thought it couldn't get worse, the glob of goo began to quiver and shake. It was moving under its own power.

Impossible. Living puke!

It shook spastically, then began to break apart like an enormous gooey egg. Out sprang a tail, followed by legs, horns, and finally a head.

Billy blinked. His jaw dropped. As the goo continued to ooze off the creature, he finally recognized what he was looking at.

"Orzamo!"

She shook the rest of the goo off and panted loudly: distressed, but not badly hurt.

"No way! The orf *swallowed* you?"

Orzamo nodded woefully. She had clearly not enjoyed her stay at the Hotel Orf. Her movements were sluggish from the effects of the orf saliva, but she obviously had a stronger natural resistance to the stuff than Billy did.

"Well, consider yourself lucky, Orzy. At least the orf didn't chew you up first."

Orzamo didn't look as if she considered herself lucky. On the contrary, her accusing stare told Billy that she was pretty ticked off about the mess he'd gotten them both into.

"Hey, I'm sorry, Orzy," said Billy. "Really. Last thing I wanted was for you to get swallowed like that. But listen: the orf is the least of our troubles. It's Twain."

Orzamo's expression turned to one of grave concern. She growled quietly.

"I'll bet you've always had your doubts about the guy."

Orzamo nodded and squinted.

Billy shot a glance at the orf. It was leaning against one of the walls, watching them with every one of its eyes. It seemed somehow less hostile, though, as if it no longer viewed Billy and Orzamo as enemies or even intruders.

Billy turned back to Orzamo.

"So here's the deal: Twain's trying to wreck the Taj Mahal. I don't know exactly why yet, but it's something to do with a beef he's got against AFMEC."

Orzamo had heard enough. She set her teeth upon Billy's detention cuff.

"Be careful now, Orzy. This thing is like . . . I don't know, nuclear-powered or something."

Orzamo ignored him. She rocked her jaws gently back and forth, manipulating the cuff with all the precision of a safe-cracker.

Billy watched the orf. It remained motionless, as if it had no intention of obstructing their escape.

After a few seconds there was a piercing mechanical squeak from the detention cuff and . . .

P'CHAK

. . . it popped open.

Billy waved his arm, tentatively at first, then with increasing confidence as he realized he was no longer in any danger of being electrocuted. He sat up, stretched his legs, and stroked Orzamo on the neck. "Nice work, Orzy. I liked you as a dog, but I *really* like you as a lizard."

Orzamo bleated an unenthusiastic note of thanks, as if she resented one version of herself being preferred over another.

Billy crossed over to the orf. He was still frightened of it, but he wanted to understand how Twain was controlling the thing. He suspected that there was more to it than just training or the threat of Twain cracking the whip.

Keeping a respectful distance, Billy examined an area just below the eyes where the fur appeared to have been cropped short. He leaned in as far as he dared and saw that there was a blinking red light there: a tiny mechanical instrument had been plunged into the orf's body like a splinter under its skin.

"Get a load of this, Orzy." Orzamo, already standing nearby, drew closer still.

"I'll bet this blinking light thingy is some kind of a torture device. Twain controls it with the button he's got attached to his belt. He can probably inflict serious pain on this orf any time he wants."

The orf blinked at Billy. For the first time Billy sensed intelligence behind the eyes, some kind of a soul lurking back there.

Billy turned back to Orzamo. "Okay. It's time for you and me to find the nearest exit." Billy cast his eyes around the cave. From what he could see, there was only one way in or out: the opening Twain had brought them through to begin with. "Let's have a look around. Maybe there's another entrance. A secret passage or something."

They spent the next ten minutes combing the walls of the cave for an alternate exit with no luck. The best they could find was a crack in one of the walls, just wide enough to squeeze through if Billy turned sideways. Orzamo jumped in and returned seconds later, shaking her head: a dead end.

"That settles it, then. We'll go out the way we came in. We might wind up bumping into Twain again, but we've gotta get back to Mom and Dad and tell them what he's up to."

Just then a noise came from somewhere in the next cave: footsteps.

Twain!

Orzamo dashed across the room and hid inside the crack in the wall. Billy froze. He wanted nothing more than to jump

Twain and wrestle him to the ground, but any fool could see who'd win the fight: Twain had all the weapons—not to mention his own personal orf—and Billy had nothing. He'd be better off waiting and seeing if he got a better chance.

Billy's eyes fell on the opened detention cuff, resting on the floor.

Don't want Twain using this *thing on me again.*

He stuffed it in his pocket, ran to the crack in the wall, and slid into the darkness just in time. He kept an eye on the orf and prayed it wouldn't blow their cover.

As the sound of the footsteps grew louder, it became clear that Twain was no longer alone. Billy peered from his hiding place and waited.

"Keep walking. And keep those hands where I can see them." Twain's voice echoed through the passageway. "Go in and sit on the floor. Both of you."

Both of you? Billy's heart sank as he realized who Twain was talking to.

Jim and Linda Clikk entered the room, hands in the air. Twain was right behind them, his pear-shaped pistol held firmly in front of him.

CHAPTER 17

Jim and Linda sat down on the floor, both wearing expressions of shock and barely contained fury. Billy could see that Twain's betrayal had caught them totally off guard. They didn't look as if they were going to put up a fight, though: they'd been stripped of their weapons.

Billy desperately wanted to come out of hiding and face Twain with them.

No. Gotta stay hidden. I can't help them until Twain's gone.

Twain looked around the room for Billy, clearly baffled. Then his eyes fell on the orf and the green goo all over the floor.

"Oh, I see." Twain walked over to the orf and wagged a disapproving finger in its face. "You ate him again, didn't you?"

Billy's parents gasped. "Billy!" Linda cried, jumping to her feet.

Twain whirled around. "On the floor!" he shouted, aiming his pear pistol straight at Linda's head. "Now!"

Linda sat back down. She had a glassy look in her eyes and her face was pale and expressionless. Jim put an arm around her shoulder. "Don't worry, honey. This isn't over yet. I'll . . . think of something. . . ."

"You're right, Jim," Twain said. "This isn't over. But it will be soon. *Very* soon." He drew a deep breath, then added: "Wrists out. Both of you."

Jim and Linda reluctantly did as they were told. Twain snapped detention cuffs on both of them.

"I don't know what you're trying to pull here, Twain," Jim said, "but you're kidding yourself if you think AFMEC won't figure it out eventually."

"Never underestimate the stupidity of AFMEC high command, Jim. I've been doing this sort of thing for years. Nothing so prominent as the Taj Mahal, of course. But you have to start small, don't you?"

Twain pulled out a small black box and attached it to a canister near the door. He then produced a mechanical device about the size and shape of a cell phone.

"A detonator," whispered Linda.

Twain smiled. "That's right, Linda. It's a good one too, I designed it myself. This button here"—he pointed to it with pride—"sends out a pulse that overpowers and disables imperm barricades. That'll come in handy when it's time to make my escape."

"Escape," said Linda, "so you can detonate the canister from a safe distance."

"That's right. Extra points if you guess what's in the canister."

"Kirradril."

Twain pursed his lips and whistled. "Very impressive. But then you always *were* the brains of the operation, weren't you, Linda? So you must be familiar with kirradril's effectiveness as a tranquilizer . . ."

". . . as well as the dangers it poses," Linda said, "due to the volatile nature of its molecular composition. Its explosive properties have resulted in AFMEC banning its use in all but the most extreme situations."

Linda paused and added: "Looks like you've got hold of an awful lot of it."

"Leftovers. From creach ops I've handled over the years."

"And just what exactly do you think you'll achieve," Linda said, "by destroying the Taj Mahal?"

"Oh, but it's not *me* destroying the Taj Mahal, Linda. It's you and your thickheaded husband here. At least, that's how it's going to look, isn't it?"

"Don't be ridiculous. No one's going to believe that we used kirradril in a simple de-creatching operation."

"But this operation turned out to be far from simple, didn't it?" Twain was pressing buttons, making sure the device in his hand could communicate with the little black box on the canister. "It's all written up in your logbook, Linda. The one they'll find in your van after this is all over. You started with floxodril. You moved up to gremadril and borradril. But none of them worked. Kirradril is the logical next step."

Twain stepped to the side of the orf and stroked its fur. "Of course, I didn't leave things to chance, Linda. I've been attending to this orf personally for the last five months. Teaching it to obey my commands. Injecting it with serum that has enhanced its natural resistance to tranquilizers of all kinds."

"But we wouldn't *resort* to kirradril!" cried Linda. "We wouldn't run the risk!"

"I know that. You know that. But Vriffnee doesn't know that. He's seen you take chances in the past. And Ravi . . . his men . . . and countries with AFMEC contracts all over the world . . . they'll be only too quick to blame the destruction of the Taj Mahal on the Clikks. And—by extension—on AFMEC itself."

"What's this all about, Twain?" Jim Clikk spoke calmly, almost in a whisper. "Your father?"

Twain squinted at Jim Clikk and jabbed a finger in his direction. "Don't . . . bring him into this."

"It's his own fault he got expelled from AFMEC, Twain. Not Vriffnee's fault. Not your fault."

Twain exploded. "My father should have been prime magistrate! And if it wasn't for Vriffnee, he *would* be!"

"Your old man was buying votes, Twain. Vriffnee blew the whistle, that's all."

"Shut up!" Twain's pear pistol was quivering in the air, just a foot or two from Jim Clikk's face.

There was an awful half minute of silence during which it seemed no one in the room knew what was going to happen next—not Billy, not Jim, not Linda, not even Twain. Then Twain exhaled, long and slow, and drew the pear pistol back.

"That's it. A few more canisters in the right spots and my work will be done. Goodbye, Jim. Goodbye, Linda." He chuckled. "You two were so well regarded at AFMEC. It's a shame this final mission of yours is going to go so . . . tragically astray."

Twain whistled to the orf and the two of them left the cave.

Billy jumped out of hiding as soon as they were gone.

"Billy!" His parents were ecstatic. Billy wanted to hug them both but feared they'd get fried from the electrical shocks.

Orzamo set to work undoing the detention cuffs while Billy apologized to his parents.

"I . . . I'm sorry, Mom and Dad. This is all my fault. If I hadn't snuck down here, you wouldn't have come after me and gotten caught by Twain."

"We would have been captured one way or another, Billy," said Jim. "Twain was well armed and waiting for us. Even if you had stayed in the tent, he would have nabbed us during our morning shift. But if you're apologizing for sneaking down here in the middle of the night after we *repeatedly* warned you how *dangerous* it was . . . well, your apology is accepted."

"I thought I could knock out the orf and be a hero," said Billy. "I was all about turning myself into a big-time creatch battler overnight."

Billy's parents wore stern expressions, but there was no disguising their relief at seeing Billy alive. "What you did was dangerous, Billy," said his father. "I think you understand that now . . ."

"I do."

". . . but it bears repeating. What you did was reckless, foolhardy, and deceitful." Jim Clikk's face softened a bit. "But I guess your mother and I have no business criticizing you for being deceitful. We kind of wrote the book on that subject, didn't we?"

Billy smiled and ran his hand through his hair. He and his parents were even now. Or near enough.

Linda, who was free from her detention cuff, gave Billy a long, warm hug. "I'm just glad you're okay, honey. Promise me . . . promise me you won't do anything like this ever again."

"I won't, Mom. I swear. Well, not until I'm an Affy-in-training, anyway."

K'CHUK

Orzamo had finished with the second cuff. They were free to go.

Jim, Linda, Billy, and Orzamo all ran from the cave and dashed through the tunnels leading back to the surface.

Everywhere they turned they came across more canisters of kirradril, each with its own black box attached, a tiny glowing orange light mounted on top, signaling that Twain could set them off at a moment's notice.

"Twain's going to blow this place sky-high!" cried Linda. "Our only chance is to get hold of him before he escapes. He won't risk activating the detonator until he's a safe distance from the Taj."

They made their way through the network of tunnels as fast as they could: sprinting through caves, scrambling up steep inclines, squeezing through narrow passageways. Their progress was agonizingly slow. Loose stones and green slime tripped them up at every turn.

We're never going to make it at this speed, Billy thought. *There's gotta be a way of covering ground faster.*

They turned one final corner and ran smack into a wall: a big, black, hairy wall.

KRRRRRRrrrrrr

"Hoh, boy," said Jim.

CHAPTER 18

The orf's eyes glinted in the darkness. It bared its teeth. Green saliva oozed to the floor. Black-furred arms rose into the air like monstrous serpents.

Linda grabbed a jagged bone from the floor of the cave and held it like a dagger. Jim did the same.

"No!" cried Billy. "I tried that. It just makes the orf angrier."

"Well, of *course* it makes the thing angrier!" shouted Jim. "But we've got to get out of here. We have no choice!"

"Let me try talking to it."

"Billy," Linda said, "orfs don't understand English."

"*This* one does," said Billy. "I've seen the way it follows Twain's orders. It *listens* to him. We might be able to get it on our side."

Jim and Linda frowned but said nothing.

"Now drop the bones. I can't talk to it if it thinks we're going to attack."

Jim turned his bone-dagger over in his hands. Then he shrugged and tossed it to the floor. Linda hesitated, then did the same. Orzamo stepped forward and placed herself just behind Billy, a look of caution and vigilance on her face.

Billy turned to the orf and placed his hand on one of its arms, sensing that his words would carry more weight if he was in physical contact with the orf. Two of the orf's other arms crept forward and snaked around Billy's waist. If it wanted to eat him, it would have him inside its mouth in a matter of seconds.

I sure hope I'm right about this.

Billy swallowed hard and peered into the orf's face. There was intelligence behind its black shiny eyes. Billy saw it clearly now.

Billy cleared his throat and spoke.

"Listen. I know what your deal is. I know what Twain has been doing to you. He's been torturing you. With *this*."

Billy pointed at the red light protruding from just below the orf's eyes.

Then he reached forward and touched it.

"He's able to hurt you with this thing, isn't he?"

The orf made its usual growling sound, only this time Billy heard it as a sympathetic sound, a sort of purring.

"You're not on Twain's side. You hate the guy just as much as I do. You only do what he says out of fear. Fear that he'll kill you."

The orf growled and hissed. *Yes, yes,* it seemed to be saying.

"When I first came down here . . . when you stuffed me into your mouth . . . you weren't even *trying* to eat me, were you?"

The orf continued making its noise. Billy's parents might have heard it as a growl, but for Billy it was now a purr. The sound hadn't changed. The way Billy was *hearing* it had.

"You were trying to *protect* me. From Twain. Hide me from him. Just like you did Orzamo."

Orzamo made an unhappy bleating noise. No doubt she wished the orf had thought up a more pleasant way of hiding her.

"All right. Twain ordered you to stay here and stop us from leaving, right? Well, think it through. If we stay here, we're all going to die, you included. The whole building's gonna be blown to bits."

The orf opened its mouth and its big black tongue lunged forward. Billy flinched, then relaxed when the orf began licking him gently on the cheek.

Jim and Linda looked on in amazement.

"See?" Billy said to his parents, letting out a big breath he didn't realize he'd been holding. "It *does* understand English."

GAAAAAAAaaaaaaaaaarrrrr

Suddenly the orf roared and jerked Billy into the air. Its arms lashed out and snatched up Jim, Linda, and Orzamo in the blink of an eye.

All was a whirl as the orf spun around, drew all of them deep into its fur, and sped off into the blackness. They all rose up and down and rocked from side to side as the orf rocketed over bumps and around tight corners. It was like riding on a tremendously fast furry roller coaster. Billy closed his eyes and held on to the orf as tightly as he could.

They barreled through the remaining tunnels in a matter of seconds. All at once they burst into the shadowy interior of the Taj Mahal, shot through one of its great stone arches, and skidded out into the gardens beyond. The sun was just beginning to peek over the trees, bathing the sky in a bright reddish orange.

Panting loudly, the orf released its grip. Jim, Linda, Orzamo, and Billy all flopped onto the ground. By the time Billy had gotten his bearings, he saw his parents and Orzamo sprinting away toward a little motorbike parked just a hundred yards from the Taj Mahal. Twain had deactivated the imperm barricade and was climbing onto the driver's seat, preparing to make his escape.

Billy immediately recognized the bike as a single-cylinder Royal Enfield Bullet 350; he'd read about them in magazines but had never seen one up close. This one was a beat-up old thing with Hindi lettering on the side and an oversized crate in the back. Billy knew its motor had originally been designed for military use, not for racing.

He won't get far. We might even catch up to him before he's reached maximum speed.

Billy jumped to his feet and rushed to join the chase. He tried to leap over a hedge, snagged his foot on a branch, and came crashing down onto the pavement. When he got back up, he was limping. Still, he did his best to run after Twain.

"Get him, Mom and Dad! Bite him on the leg, Orzy!"

Twain revved the engine and tore across one of the garden paths leading out of the Taj Mahal complex. Jim and Linda tried to run after him, but it was no use. He was several yards ahead of them and gaining ground.

It was up to Orzamo now. She charged after Twain at top speed. Within seconds she was just a few feet from the rear of the motorcycle. One good jump and she would have him.

"Come on, Orzy. You can do it. . . ."

That was when Twain kicked the motorcycle into a higher gear.

More than just a higher gear, actually.

This was a gear that most bikers can only dream about: the wheels left the ground and Twain rose gracefully into the air.

No!

Twain's beat-up motorbike was tricked out with AFMEC transgravitational propulsion. With each passing second it climbed higher into the air. Orzamo slowed to a trot and barked at the top of her lungs.

There's got to be some way of stopping him, thought Billy.

Twain banked the motorbike to one side and soared back over their heads, flaunting his freedom.

"*Sayonara*, folks!" he cried, holding the detonator above his head like a trophy. "And buh-bye, Taj Mahal!"

Twain's mocking farewell made Billy even angrier than he had been.

I've gotta get up there and stop him. Somehow . . .

Twain hovered above them for a moment, then revved the motorcycle's engine and began to speed away into the early-morning clouds.

I've got it: the orf!

Billy ran to the orf's side and grabbed one of its tentacles.

"Throw me!" he cried. "Come on, it's our only chance!"

The orf snapped one of its black furry arms around Billy's waist and drew him back like a pitcher winding up for a fastball.

You better be as accurate as the book said, thought Billy, *or I'm dead meat.*

Billy caught a brief glimpse of the orf's glimmering eyes before he was hurled into the sky. If he had been fired from a cannon, he couldn't have flown any faster. Even on his best days of snowboarding he'd never experienced anything like this.

Everything seemed to move in slow motion as Billy tumbled through the air, the Taj Mahal spiraling away below him, the wind whipping his hair all over the place. It was like his best dream and his worst nightmare all in one. He was having visions of his body crashing through the roof of some Indian family's living room when . . .

FOOOMPF

"Nnnnggggghh!"

He blinked and looked around. He was right behind Twain's back, seated sideways in the motorbike's crate, soaring over the rooftops of Agra.

CHAPTER 19

The cool morning wind stung Billy's skin as he peered down at the buildings rushing by beneath him. Red-tiled rooftops and leafy trees, Hindu temples and traffic-packed boulevards, back-street gardens and empty marketplaces . . . It was a dizzying sight: spectacular and horrifying at the same time. Billy thanked his lucky stars he wasn't scared of heights.

Twain was speechless. He was also angry. His face was burning red with rage and his teeth were bared like the fangs of a rabid dog.

He jammed the detonator into his breast pocket and tried to dislodge Billy with his free hand. "Get off this bike, you little punk!" The bike lurched to one side. Though Twain had only one free arm to fight, he was using the motorbike to full advantage:

every time Billy moved to attack, Twain spun the bike sideways, leaving Billy scrambling to avoid a fall.

Billy held on for dear life. Twain elbowed him. Kicked him. He probably would have bitten him if he could have managed it. The merciless wind and the unpredictable movements of the bike only compounded the difficulty of staying in the crate. Still Billy held on.

When Twain grabbed him by the hair, Billy thrust his hand out and tried to grab the detonator. He nearly got hold of it before Twain turned away and drew a zipper shut over the pocket.

"Oh no you don't!"

Twain then began trying to dislodge Billy by other means. Billy kept a close eye on him as Twain gripped the handlebars with both hands.

Throwing his body weight to one side, Twain flipped the motorbike completely upside down.

Billy's whole body jerked off the bike and he nearly lost his grip. Without a second to spare, he latched on to the exhaust pipe and held on with all his might. The pipe was warm but not yet scalding hot. Billy gazed down in horror as the city of Agra raced by hundreds of feet below him.

Don't let go don't let go don't let go

"Why . . . won't . . . you . . . FALL?"

Twain sent the bike into a stomach-churning corkscrew. Everything turned into a whirling blur.

Billy held on to the exhaust pipe, clenching his fingers around it.

After what must have been a dozen spins, Twain leveled the bike off and growled with frustration.

"All right!" He unzipped his breast pocket. "I'll deal with you later." He pulled out the detonator.

No! He's going to set it off NOW!

Billy climbed up and grabbed hold of Twain's arm. Twain elbowed Billy back and flipped open a protective cover on the detonator. Beneath it was a numerical keypad. Twain clearly would have preferred having two hands free to work the thing, but he needed one arm to hold the bike steady.

Billy tried again to snatch the detonator out of Twain's hand. This time Twain elbowed him right in the face, sending him tumbling back into the delivery basket.

"Nngh!"

By the time Billy got back up, Twain was already punching a sequence of numbers into the detonator.

Billy grabbed Twain's arm with both hands. The bike wobbled wildly in the air.

"Drop it, Twain!" he shouted. *"Drop. It!"*

Billy didn't get the detonator out of Twain's hand, but he at least managed to make him push the wrong buttons.

"You little freak!" cried Twain. "Now I've got to start all over again!"

Twain elbowed Billy once more in the face. This time it really hurt. Billy was running out of stamina, and running out of hope. It was only a matter of time before Twain would punch in the right sequence of numbers and the Taj Mahal would be gone.

Billy made one more grab for the detonator and got one more elbow in the face. The bike rocked violently.

This isn't working. There's got to be some other way to stop him . . .

Stop him . . .

The detention cuff!

Billy reached into his pocket. There it was, just where he'd put it when he'd hidden from Twain in the cave.

He pulled it out, opened it, leaped up, and snapped it around Twain's wrist.

FZZZIIIIIITCH!

"Yaaaaaah!"

Twain's fingers splayed spastically as he tried to maintain his grip on the detonator. Billy reached out, pulled it from Twain's hand, and tucked it safely into his own pocket. The bike started spinning chaotically through the air and—even worse—began to lose altitude.

Now comes the tough part.

Moving as quickly as he could, Billy began pulling Twain's tense body back into the crate. He grabbed Twain by the shoulders and heaved him backward, the bike rocking crazily all the while. Twain howled with every move, the detention cuff shooting relentless shock waves through his body. When Billy went to move Twain's legs, he nearly ended up throwing him off the bike entirely: only a last-second save by Billy kept Twain from freefalling all the way down into the streets of Agra. It took every last ounce of energy Billy had—and a further loss of precious altitude—but at last he got Twain where he wanted him. Panting and wiping the sweat from his face, Billy took his place in the driver's seat.

Billy knew all about riding motorbikes, but being behind the controls of a *flying* motorbike was definitely a first. Fortunately it turned out to be pretty simple: he turned the handlebars in the direction he wanted to go, and the bike took him there. There was a lever for altitude, but otherwise it was pretty similar to all the motorcycle video games Billy had played over the years. Soon the Taj Mahal was back in his field of vision.

Twain groaned and bellowed as they made their way back. He even made a few desperate attempts to interfere with Billy's steering. But the detention cuff was—as Twain himself had said—in good working order. After two or three electrical shocks so powerful they frightened passing birds, Twain finally collapsed into the delivery basket and became as timid as a baby in a crib. The rest of the flight was uneventful.

When he steered the bike down into the Taj Mahal complex, Billy realized that the brake pedal wasn't working properly. He managed to slow the bike down, but there was no way he'd be able to bring it to a complete stop.

Gotta improvise.

He pointed the bike in the direction of the largest, leafiest tree in the complex and hoped its branches weren't as hard as they looked. Within seconds it grew from a tree in the distance to a big, blurred wall of leaves.

"Yaaaaaaaaa!"

"Billy!" he heard his parents cry just before he, Twain, and the bike plunged into the treetop. Billy flew off the driver's seat, barreled through thirty feet of leaves and branches, and somersaulted out the other side. Flailing his arms and legs in all directions, he tumbled into the middle of a large hedge at the border of a nearby walkway.

A few seconds later, after Jim and Linda pulled Billy out and carried him to a soft patch of grass nearby, they found him in a wretched state. His head, neck, arms, and hands were scraped and cut in more places than could be counted. He was bruised. He was battered. He was bleeding.

He was also smiling.

"I did it," he said. "I saved the Taj Mahal."

The worried expressions on his parents' faces gave way to big toothy grins.

"That you did, my boy," said Jim. "That you did."

Linda leaned over and found one of the few unscratched places on Billy's cheek to plant a kiss. She tried to say something but ended up just shaking her head and laughing in a way that was hard to distinguish from crying.

CHAPTER 20

With the help of Ravi Goswami and his men, Jim Clikk re-
trieved Twain and his motorbike from the top of the tree. Twain
was bad shape too, maybe even worse than Billy.

Billy watched as his father held Twain down and snapped
an extra detention cuff on him for good measure.

"Would your father really have approved of any of this,
Twain?" asked Jim. "He was crooked, but at least he knew whose
side he was on."

Twain ignored this remark. "You haven't seen the last of
me, Clikk!" he growled. "They won't keep me locked up forever.
I'll be back. And remember," he added, training his eyes on
Billy, "I know where you live."

A large squadron of Affys had arrived not long after Billy's

dramatic return, and now they took Twain into custody. The last Billy saw of him was his struggling body being carried into an AFMEC transport vehicle disguised as an Indian garbage truck.

"So Twain was a mole," said Billy. "He was trying to bring AFMEC down from the inside."

"Hard to believe, isn't it?" Jim put his arm around Billy's shoulder and they walked slowly through the gardens together. "He was one of the hardest-working Affys of them all. I thought it was all in the service of clearing the family name. Now I can see he was obsessed with one thing and one thing only: wreaking vengeance upon Mr. Vriffnee and the entire AFMEC organization.

"See, there's been a slew of Affy creatch ops that have ended disastrously in the last few years," said Jim. "I'll bet Twain had a hand in all of them. Imagine if he'd succeeded in destroying the Taj Mahal and blaming it on AFMEC." Jim grimaced. "I don't think the organization could have recovered from something like that."

"Do you think agents got killed because of Twain?"

Jim paused before answering. "I don't know. It's certainly possible. You can be sure AFMEC will be conducting a thorough investigation to find out."

"What's going to happen to him now? Will he go to jail?"

"There's a facility for agents like him in AFMECopolis. He'll get a chance to start over again, to reform himself and rejoin regular society. But he's going to be stripped of his Affy status—just like his father was—for life. And AFMEC will be keeping an eye on him until he's old and gray, you can bank on that."

"So what's his real name?" asked Billy. "Not Twain, right?"

Jim snickered. "Orville Q. Lumpkins."

"Ooh. No *wonder* he chose a code name."

Jim and Billy walked—limped, in Billy's case—back to the plaza surrounding the Taj Mahal. There they found that Linda had injected the orf with a local anesthetic in preparation for removing Twain's remote-control torture device. At her feet was a case containing an array of scalpels and other surgical tools. Linda had also made an important discovery, which she announced to them both in an excited whisper.

"She's pregnant."

Billy's eyes widened. "The orf? No way! I thought it was a guy."

"Yeah, well, it's kinda hard to tell, isn't it?" The giant black beast groaned as Linda began making the necessary incisions. "I should have known by the change in eye color. Pregnant creatches have darker eyes. They also experience a dramatic rise in intelligence during the months prior to childbirth. It's an evolutionary quirk: a temporary change in brain chemistry that allows the creatch to choose the best possible place in which to raise her offspring, thereby ensuring the survival of the species."

"I get it," said Billy. "So Twain went looking for a pregnant creatch to begin with, one that would be smart enough for him to train."

"That's right. Between Twain's knowledge of creatch behavior in general and this little remote-control 'cattle prod,' he had everything he needed to turn this orf into his own personal servant. He just didn't count on the increased sense of compassion that came with the orf's boost in intelligence. The orf feared the suffering Twain was able to inflict on her, but—as you discovered—she never really wanted to hurt anyone."

"Wow. So what are we going to do with it . . . I mean, *her* . . . now that the mission's over?"

"She's a ground creatch, Billy. She belongs in her natural habitat deep beneath the earth. The only time orfs come to the surface is when there's a subterranean crisis like an earthquake. Or when a creep like Twain drags them into one of his crackpot schemes."

"You mean Orville Q. Lumpkins?" Billy grinned.

"Don't make fun of people's names, Billy," said Linda. "It's not nice."

Billy took a long last look at the orf. Even in broad daylight, she was a pretty fearsome beast: big, hairy, sharp-toothed monsters are pretty intimidating no matter how friendly or pregnant they may be. But it was also a thrill to be standing next to something so huge and otherworldly.

My first creatch op, thought Billy. *Sure as heck won't be my last, though.*

"Take care," he said, reaching up to pat its head.

The orf opened its mouth and belched loudly. Out came the same cloud of greenish brown smoke and its accompanying awful stench.

"Ugh. Don't take this personally, but all in all, you staying miles beneath the earth's surface is not a bad thing."

Minutes later the orf crawled back into the Taj Mahal, where it disappeared into the hole, tunneled back down to the world it had come from, and, presumably, got ready to start a nice big orf family.

Within minutes Ravi Goswami's crew of artisans were hard at work filling in the hole and restoring the Taj Mahal to its former glory.

"Thank you once again, Mr. and Mrs. Clikk," said Ravi as one of his assistants brought around glasses of chai on a tray. "And thank *you,* Billy. You have proven every bit as resourceful as your parents. The family business is in good hands. I strongly recommend, however," he added, motioning toward the severely damaged tree behind him, "that you investigate other means of landing a flying motorbike."

TEEP

Jim Clikk pulled out his viddy-fone.

"Yes, Mr. Vriffnee . . ."

"Thank you, Mr. Vriffnee. It was our pleasure."

"Well, nothing that time and a few dozen bandages won't heal."

"Yes, he's right here beside me."

"Certainly."

Jim Clikk handed the viddy-fone to his son.

Billy's heart beat faster as he held the viddy-fone in his palm. He'd been wanting a new cell phone for ages (his parents refused to buy him a new one after he smashed his Motorola to pieces while skateboarding down the steps of the Piffling Public Library). Now, though, peering into the paper-thin blue video screen resting in his hand, he knew he could never settle for anything less than his own viddy-fone.

Mr. Vriffnee, his face no more than an inch from top to bottom, was staring out at him. He was frowning.

"Highly irregular what you did today, young man. I don't even want to *count* how many AFMEC rules you violated."

Billy swallowed.

"I shudder to think what kind of mess we'd be in if every Affy's kid started behaving like you do. You have shown a blatant disregard for AFMEC procedure every step of the way."

Billy swallowed again.

"You have also helped to save AFMEC—to say nothing of the Taj Mahal—from a very serious threat."

Billy was too stunned to smile. He just stood there like a statue: a statue with a viddy-fone in its hand.

"And for that I thank you."

Billy knew he had remained silent for too long. "I . . . I don't know what to say, sir."

Mr. Vriffnee's mouth moved in the direction of a smile.

"I think *you're welcome* is the usual response."

"You're welcome, sir."

"And stop calling me sir. You can't get out of mispronouncing my name *that* easily."

Billy felt his face grow warm. Jim and Linda chuckled.

"That's all for now, Billy. Your parents will be bringing you back to AFMECopolis shortly. First comes the cleanup operation."

"Yes, Mr. Vriffnee."

"Normally in these circumstances I would force you to do it alone. Today, however—by special request—I am sending an Affy out to assist you. She'll be there shortly."

She?

CHAPTER 21

Ana García arrived within half an hour. She had asked permission to help Billy with his first cleanup operation, and Mr. Vriffnee, in recognition of the fine work she and her parents had just completed in Vladivostok, granted her wish.

"You can't just move the brush back and forth like that, you know," she said. They were washing green goo off the floors of the Taj Mahal using buckets, scrub brushes, and a special AFMEC-developed detergent that came in surprisingly ordinary-looking spray bottles. It was the hottest part of the day, and even the shadows of the Taj weren't enough to keep them both from sweating profusely. "Circular motions work best. Trust me. I've had to do a *lot* of this the last few years."

It was the kind of comment that would have driven Billy

up the wall the first time he met her. It still did, actually. Just slightly less so, for some reason.

"So, Ana," said Billy, "do you think they'll make me a full-time Affy like you? I mean, come on. I saved this place from getting blown to bits. That's gotta count for something."

"You don't know AFMEC like I do, Billy." Ana grunted as she worked at a particularly difficult stain. "You could have saved the entire planet and they'd still check the books to make sure you followed the right procedures. If you're really lucky," she added, "they'll put you on track to become an Affy-in-training within the next six months."

"Six *months*?" Billy dunked his brush into his bucket so forcefully he created a small waterfall of suds. "Jeez, no wonder Twain had it in for these guys. Maybe I should switch sides."

Ana chuckled. "I know. Sometimes I think being a creatch would be a lot more fun. I know some kids at school I wouldn't mind chewing up and spitting out."

"Whoa," said Billy with an exaggerated expression of shock. "You're scarin' me here, Ana. Good thing I'm your friend and not your enemy."

Ana laughed out loud. "You don't know the half of it. I've been through AFMEC hand-to-hand combat training. I could break you in two right now if I wanted." She smiled, but Billy sensed it was no lie.

"Dang," he said, scrubbing with renewed vigor, "I've got a lot of work ahead of me."

"*Oh* yeah."

Several hours later Billy, Ana, and both of their families flew back to AFMECopolis. There they joined an intimate group of high-ranking Affys who had gathered for a small ceremony at one end of Vigilance Park, a leafy expanse of green at the center of the vast underwater complex. A small wooden stage stood before two rows of folding chairs and a table topped by a punch bowl and three platters of vita-dogs, hypersprouts, and dozens of other dishes packed with vitamins, minerals, and very little flavor.

Jim, Linda, and Billy sat in the front row. They were wearing fresh AFMEC uniforms, and Billy's wounds were neatly bandaged, having been dressed by a nurse at the towering AFMEC medical complex half an hour before. ("Orf saliva and mulberry leaves," she'd said as she cleaned Billy up. "Interesting combination.") Seated in the second row were Fernando García and his family, along with a dozen other Affys Billy had just been introduced to.

The small group quieted as Mr. Vriffnee strode up to the stage and tested the podium's microphone.

TUP TUP TUP

"Good afternoon."

Billy sat up straight. It wasn't easy to do—his scratches and bruises still stung pretty badly—but this was not an occasion to slouch through.

"My fellow Affys. I'm sure you're all familiar with the story of Antonio Valoroso, the great fourteenth-century Italian creatch battler who saved the Tower of Pisa—in the very nick of time—from being toppled by a band of renegade amphibious sea creatches.

"Today we have before us a group of people who have done something every bit as remarkable. They have saved the Taj Mahal from ruin and ferreted out one of the most heinous double agents ever to infiltrate this organization. Would you please join me in welcoming to this stage the Clikk family: Jim, Linda, Billy, and their adopted demi-creatch, Orzamo."

There was a quiet but warm round of applause as Jim and Linda rose, followed by Billy and Orzamo.

"Now, before we have you all say a few words," said Mr. Vriffnee, adjusting the microphone's height for Billy, "there's a little something I'd like to present to Billy on behalf of the entire organization."

Louise, the frumpy-looking secretary from the elevator video screen, stepped forward from the audience and handed something to Mr. Vriffnee. It was like a miniature briefcase, made of lacquered cherry wood with brass fittings. A plaque on one side was etched with bold letters:

BILLY CLIKK
AFMEC
AGENT-IN-TRAINING

Mr. Vriffnee unlocked the clasps and opened the case, revealing a velvety green interior housing three objects: the detention cuff he'd used to defeat Twain, a leather-bound book (*The Agent's Guide to AFMEC Rules and Regulations*), and a brand-new viddy-fone.

"It gives me great pleasure," said Mr. Vriffnee, "to welcome to the fold our newest AFMEC trainee."

Billy shot a glance at Ana in the audience. She winked, and Billy realized—with both embarrassment and relief—that she'd been in on the whole thing: the "six-month wait" had been her way of throwing him off the trail.

"If this young man is anything like his parents," continued Vriffnee, "and I'm afraid it's painfully clear that he is, at least as far as *rule breaking* goes"—

A smattering of laughter from the audience.

—"he will one day make a very fine Affy indeed."

Mr. Vriffnee shook Billy's hand again, gave him the heavy wooden case, and invited him to step forward to the podium.

Billy snuck a quick glance at the expectant faces before him but found that it only made him more nervous. Some of the Affys in the audience wore rows of glittering pins and medals on their uniforms, evidence of their high rank within the organization. A few of the men had long bushy beards, making them look like battle-hardened ship captains.

"Thank—"

KEEEEEEEeeeeeeeeee

A shriek of feedback from the microphone.

"Thank you, Mr. Vriffnee. I, uh, feel really lucky . . . to, uh . . . to be here today."

The way he said it, people in the audience might have thought he meant he felt fortunate simply to still be alive. Heck, he *did* mean that, come to think of it.

"There are three people I need to thank. Actually, two people and one demi-creatch." A few chuckles from the audience. "Thanks to my mom and dad. You two are the best parents a guy could hope for."

His parents smiled and joined hands.

"Now that I've seen some of the different kinds of weapons

you have at your disposal, I'm, uh . . . *really* glad you've never done anything worse than send me to my room."

The crowd laughed loudly.

"I, uh, also have to thank this amazing demi-creatch here"—he gestured to Orzamo—"who until a couple of days ago was just another Scottish terrier, and a pretty lazy one at that."

More laughter. Billy looked directly at Orzamo. She had her snout held high, but her tail was moving in a jittery way that suggested she was suffering a minor case of stage fright. "She's the real hero here. If not for her, I'd be dead and the Taj Mahal would be history. Thank you, Orzy. Thank you for everything."

Billy was about to step away from the microphone, but then it dawned on him that he'd forgotten something. Or someone. Someone very important.

"I, uh . . . I need to thank someone who isn't here today. She can't be here today because she lives miles and miles underground. She's an orf, and, uh . . . I don't even know her name. Maybe she doesn't even *have* a name. But she was an important part of this mission. Maybe the most important part. And what she did needs to be . . . appreciated."

People in the audience looked confused. Affys didn't normally say nice things about creatches in the middle of acceptance speeches.

"Thank you, Mrs. Orf, wherever you are right now. I hope you have lots of kids and . . . and live a nice, long . . . orfy life."

It was an odd way to end the speech. But one or two Affys started clapping, more joined in, and finally the whole audience was on its feet.

Billy bowed as deeply as he could bear to and limped back to where his parents were standing.

Jim and Linda, beaming with pride, indicated that they had nothing to add, and Vriffnee returned to the microphone.

"All right then, enough of this idle chatter," he said, adopting a gruff tone that was probably only half in jest: "Back to work, all of you!"

CHAPTER 22

The Clikk family ended up getting a vacation after all. When they arrived back home early Monday morning, Jim Clikk phoned Piffling Elementary and explained that Billy would be joining them in South Carolina for a week, visiting his ailing grandmother. Which turned out to be true. (Well, everything but the ailing part.) They spent the rest of Monday, Tuesday, Wednesday, and the better part of Thursday doing nothing but lounging around Gramma Clikk's house, a creaky old place near the beach, half hidden in weeds at the dead end of a dirt road.

Billy soon realized that his mother hadn't been kidding when she'd referred to Gramma Clikk's head-spinning stories. By Thursday afternoon Billy's grandmother had told him about forest creatches she had battled deep in the jungles of Peru, mountain creatches she'd slain single-handedly (waist deep in snow on the plateaus of Tibet), and sky creatches she'd gone head to head with in a battle-scarred biplane worthy of the Red Baron.

Right now, though, Gramma Clikk was in the middle of her late-afternoon nap. Jim, Linda, Billy, and Orzamo (back in Scottish terrier form) were lazing on the beach, listening to the surf and occasionally making suggestions as to what they should have for dinner that night.

"How about seafood?" asked Jim.

"Mmm," said both Billy and Linda.

"I hear that diner in town has pretty good salmon."

"That reminds me, Dad," Billy said, picking at a scab on his knee, "what were all those salmon heads for? You know, the ones you bought in Nome."

"Oh, that." Jim Clikk was flat on his back, expending as little energy as possible. "That was for Nessie."

"Nessie. You mean, like, *Loch Ness Monster* Nessie?"

"Don't ask me what she was doing off the coast of Alaska. All I know is we needed the salmon heads to lure her out of Nome Harbor and lead her back to sea. We had a devil of a time getting her out of there without the locals catching on. This one reporter from the *Nome Nugget*—that's the local paper—boy, she was a handful, let me tell ya."

"So did the salmon heads work?"

Linda Clikk, who was in the middle of a romance novel—a *real* romance novel—answered the question before her husband could: "No, of *course* they didn't work. Every Affy knows Nessie prefers rainbow trout. . . ."

"Look," Jim said, "they were *out* of rainbow trout, so I got the salmon heads. I mean, come on. . . ."

TEEP

Jim Clikk jumped up to a sitting position, as if he'd just heard a siren. Billy rose to his elbows. *The viddy-fone.*

Linda gave her husband a disapproving look. "Honey, I thought you said you turned that thing off."

"I did. You know, from Monday through Wednesday. But I figured today I'd switch it on . . . just in case."

TEEP

Jim Clikk fished the viddy-fone from a nearby duffel bag and popped it open. The familiar Vriffnee growl came blasting out.

A new creach op, thought Billy. *It's gotta be.*

Jim Clikk sat up straight and rubbed some sand out of his eyes. "I'm sorry, Mr. Vriffnee."

Another blast of Vriffnee anger.

"Yes, but we *are* on vacation. . . ."

"I understand that, Mr. Vriffnee, but . . ."

"Yes . . ."

Billy's heart was thumping. Here he was, still bruised and

bandaged from his first mission. But he was ready for another one. He was *ready*.

"Certainly."

"The monastery of Erdene Zuu? I've *heard* of it, yes, but . . ."

"Well, yes, of *course* Linda speaks Mongolian, Mr. Vriffnee, but . . ."

Definitely a new mission. But will I be included? Or will Mr. Vriffnee say I need more time to recuperate?

"I see."

"And should we bring Billy along, or . . ."

Please say yes please say yes please say yes . . .

"Okay."

"Okay." Jim Clikk shot Billy an apologetic glance. "Well, he's going to be disappointed to hear that, but . . ."

Billy's heart sank.

"Thank you, Mr. Vriffnee. We'll be there as soon as possible."

TEEP

Jim turned to Billy with a tired smile. "Vacation's over, son. Skeeter gig. In Mongolia."

Billy was devastated. He already knew the answer, but he asked the question anyway: "Did Mr. Vriffnee say I could come along?"

"No."

Jim Clikk snapped the viddy-fone shut and grinned.

"He said you *must* come along."

"*Really?*" Billy was on his feet.

"Of *course*. You're an Affy-in-training now, kiddo. You need all the practice you can get."

Within fifteen minutes Jim, Linda, Billy, and Orzamo had kissed Gramma Clikk goodbye and piled into the van. Before his father had even put the keys in the ignition, Billy had fired up one of the computers to begin researching the creatches—a herd of five-headed gargazaks, according to his father—that were waiting for them in Mongolia.

Mongolia. Man, this is gonna be sweet. They're, like, really into horses in Mongolia, aren't they? Maybe we'll have to fight these gargazaks while riding horseback across the steppes. . . .

Soon they were rumbling down the bumpy dirt road leading back to the highway. Of course, they had no intention of actually getting *on* the highway.

As the wheels left the road and the van soared off into the sky, Billy closed his eyes and smiled, knowing that his life would never be THE USUAL again.

About the Author

Mark Crilley is a senior member of AFMECT (the American Federation of Moderately Eccentric Creative Types), an affiliation his wife was not aware of when she agreed to marry him. A graduate of Kalamazoo College, he taught English in Taiwan and Japan for five years, during which time he never battled anything more frightening than a bad cold. Crilley is the author and illustrator of the Akiko series of comic books and novels for young readers and is a regular contributor to *Nickelodeon Magazine.* He lives in Michigan with his wife, Miki, and son, Matthew, who is extremely fond of monsters, as all good children should be.

Visit the author at www.markcrilley.com.